10/02

D1563824

PASSAGE TO
DODGE CITY

**Center Point
Large Print**

**This Large Print Book carries the
Seal of Approval of N.A.V.H.**

ॐ श्री गणेशाय नमः

PASSAGE TO DODGE CITY

RAY HOGAN

CENTER POINT PUBLISHING
THORNDIKE, MAINE

This Center Point Large Print edition
is published in the year 2002 by arrangement with
Golden West Literary Agency.

The text of this Large Print edition is unabridged. In other
aspects, this book may vary from the original edition. Printed in
Thailand. Set in 16-point Times New Roman type by
Bill Coskrey and Gary Socquet.

ISBN 1-58547-239-5

Library of Congress Cataloging-in-Publication Data.

Hogan, Ray, 1908-
    Passage to Dodge City / Ray Hogan.--Center Point large print ed.
        p. cm.
    ISBN 1-58547-239-5 (lib. bdg. : alk. paper)
    1. Large type books. I. Title.

PS3558.O3473 P38 2002
813'.54--dc21   2002067203

PASSAGE TO DODGE CITY

1

Tucson was another bust. Starbuck had hung around the old Arizona mission town for a full week hoping to learn something of his missing brother, Ben, to no avail. No one had seen or heard of a man answering the meager description Shawn could give.

Earlier he had come close; Ben had been in Silver City, had staged a boxing match there for the citizens of that wild, free-spending little mining town, and had ridden on—only hours before Starbuck, delayed by an obligation he felt he could not ignore, had arrived. The incident had provided one gainful result, however; he now knew definitely that Ben was also calling himself Damon Friend.

So far as he was aware, that was the nearest he had ever come to finding the brother for whom he'd searched so long; and the dismal knowledge that he had been on the very brink of ending the chase and settling the family matters that would enable him to forsake the endless trails and build a life of his own—only to fail—was a bitter conclusion to a soaring hope.

His persistent quest had carried him ceaselessly back and forth across the frontier, from the Mexican border to Canada, from the Mississippi to the California coast, always with no luck. Several times he had thought himself near success, only to have the person believed to be Ben turn out a stranger, or perhaps, as was the case in Silver City, already gone.

But on that occasion, in the brawling New Mexico settlement where silver was king, it had been different; Ben actually had been there and only circumstances had prevented the long-sought-for meeting that was so important to Shawn.

He had thought Ben would head for Tucson after that. The ancient Arizona town was said to be booming, and it was a logical place for a man looking for work. Again he guessed wrong; there were jobs to be had but Ben was not, nor had he been, among those seeking to sign on.

When it became apparent Shawn was only wasting time there, he had swung north, remembering the big ranchers in what was known as the Rockinstraw Valley country; this was the season when they would be adding hired hands. A seemingly reliable tip had taken him there once before, but the lead, like all the others he had followed, had proven to be of no value.

Once more failure was his only reward; there was no trace of Ben, and the long side trip had developed into little more than a renewal of friendships started during his original visit. Now, slumped in the saddle of the big sorrel gelding he rode, he gave thought to his next destination as he slowly made his way across the forsaken Sulphur Springs flats.

El Paso, he supposed, indifferently, and then perhaps across the line into Juarez and on down into Mexico if he had no luck in the pass city some folks still referred to as Magoffansville. One place seemed as good a bet as another; Ben could be anywhere.

Raising a hand, Starbuck brushed at the sweat blurring his narrowed eyes. It was early summer and the glaring heat had already set in. It would be hot in El Paso, too, as

8

well as on the other side of the Rio Grande, he knew, but the realization brought only a shrug to his shoulders. He had long since reached that stage where he accepted things beyond his power to change—such as time and the elements—as no more or no less than pure reality, a fact of life that a man must accommodate to and make the best of.

He glanced ahead to a maze of low, rolling, brush-covered hills. There was a settlement somewhere beyond them; to the south, he thought. With a bit of luck he should reach it by nightfall. Shawn hoped so. The ragged land into which he was riding would offer little in the way of a decent campsite.

Reaching the first of the bluffs, he again wiped at the sweat on his face, and raising himself in his stirrups, looked to the south. A tall, lean man, he appeared to be all bone and muscle in the harsh sunlight, and his deep-set gray-blue eyes, overshadowed by dark, thick brows seemed colorless at that moment.

Young in years by the prescribed standard of numerical count, he nevertheless possessed the calm sureness which only crystallizing experience can bestow upon a man and fill him with that indefinable quality of cold self-sufficiency so necessary in a savage land where only the quick and the wise stay alive.

His glance rested upon a paloverde tree, a faded green blur on the burned flat. He'd best start veering toward it, more to the south, he decided, resuming his seat and putting the gelding into motion. The town he now recalled was just beyond the peaks at the end of the mountains to his left—the Swisshelms, someone had told him they were called. The name of the settlement he could not remember; a Mexican word, it seemed. Whatever, it was of no great consequence, only that it was there and—

The high, sharp crack of a pistol, a quick spurt of sand a dozen strides beyond the sorrel, brought Starbuck up short. Startled and angry, he glanced around, scanning the countless rolling mounds of brush-covered brown earth.

Had that bullet been meant for him? It hadn't come close, seemed more a stray shot—and who would be gunning for him? He could think of no one at the moment. Apaches? It wasn't likely. Indians seldom used pistols, generally preferring a rifle or a shotgun.

There was no one in sight. A stray bullet, he concluded, possibly directed his way by ricochet. Settling back, Shawn touched the gelding with his spurs, and moved on. Likely it had been some passing pilgrim or cowhand beyond the humps of land taking a shot at a gopher or some other varmint.

The pistol cracked again. Starbuck felt the breath of the bullet, heard the rattle of it as it clipped through a clump of sun-dried mesquite behind him. He reacted as the echoes began to roll, roweling the sorrel sharply, sending him plunging ahead. The six gun's report sounded once more, that bullet striking well ahead of the gelding. There was no doubt now; someone was shooting at him—someone, fortunately, not too skilled with a weapon.

Bent low over the sorrel's neck, Shawn swerved his horse toward an arroyo some fifty yards farther on. It appeared deep and could offer protection. Again the pistol crackled. Sand spurted up at the gelding's front hooves, sent him shying to the left. The shots were coming from somewhere to the south, Starbuck realized, and instantly swung the sorrel to the opposite direction, thus presenting a more difficult target. Another report blasted through the afternoon's heat and then another.

Six times, Starbuck thought grimly as the gelding thundered on toward the deep cut. *A man who carried a full cylinder in his weapon.* He would have to reload now unless he had a second gun—or there was more than one bushwhacker.

The arroyo was suddenly before him. The sorrel hesitated briefly, sprang, and then he was down in its sandy depth.

Starbuck left the saddle the instant his horse righted himself. He hit the ground running, rushed forward to the edge of the arroyo, and shielded by a clump of rabbit-bush, threw his glance in the direction from which the shots had come.

He could see no one, hear no sound. By that moment the bushwhacker would have had time to reload and be ready to try his luck again—but now it would be different; now they were on even terms.

Shawn continued to sweep the brushy, rolling land before him with studied care. Nothing. Was the would-be-killer, apparently in an arroyo also, working his way around, hoping to circle and come in from behind? And who the hell was he? Starbuck swore in exasperation.

What was it all about? Robbery?

Again his mind went back to the Apaches. There were plenty of Chiricahuas in the area, some friendly, others openly hostile. That they didn't ordinarily use a handgun was no absolute guarantee that they would not. It could be a party of renegades after his horse and weapons, but he still doubted it.

Mexican bandits. That seemed a more likely possibility. Bands of the fierce, bandoliered riders crossed the border regularly to raid wagon trains and stagecoaches, attacking solitary travelers on the way. He shook his head; that idea didn't bear up either. There was only one gun, therefore only a lone man. The Mexicans, like the Apaches, ran in packs.

He pulled back, eyes aching from staring steadily into the glare. High above the quiet, sprawling country, an eagle lifted and fell gracefully as he rode the air currents in search of prey below. Starbuck, hunched low, moved another ten yards farther along the wash to a second clump of brush. From that new vantage point he again scanned the unfriendly land before him.

Nothing . . . only the soaring eagle etching the clean, blue sky overhead. He wheeled impatiently. The bushwhacker had either given up or was waiting for him to mount and once more show himself on high ground. Whoever it was, he'd be wasting his time, Starbuck decided. He'd keep down in the arroyo, not expose—

Shawn halted. The sorrel, standing a few strides farther on, had looked up quickly. Long neck curved, he was staring over his shoulder, watching the upper end of the wash.

Left hand dropping to the forty-five on his hip, Starbuck crossed quickly to the opposite side of the cut, where a bulge of root-filled earth jutted out. He had heard nothing, but the sorrel had detected a sound or had perhaps picked up an odor with his sensitive nostrils. Something had attracted him—and Shawn had never known the big gelding to be wrong.

The moments dragged. Nearby a striped lizard appeared on the edge of the arroyo's bank, eyed Starbuck briefly, and crawled on toward a flat of rock in short, jerky movements. The sorrel continued to watch the upper end of the wash, lowering his head only now and then to tear at the dry grass beneath him.

Sound registered on Starbuck's straining ears—the slow thud of a walking horse, the faint creak of leather. Shortly, a man leading his mount stepped into view.

He was up in years, in his sixties, Shawn guessed as he considered the stranger critically. Dressed in ordinary range clothing—checked shirt, vest, cord pants, boots that were badly scarred, and a hat with a sagging brim—he was looking intently ahead. Evidently he could see the sorrel, was endeavoring to locate its rider.

Starbuck remained hidden behind the shoulder of sod, moving nearer to it for closer scrutiny. The man looked tough. Hawk-faced, he had small, dark eyes, and a head capped by a shock of bushy white hair that contrasted oddly with thick dark brows and mustache.

"Hello—there in the wash!"

Starbuck did not reply. He continued to study the man, searching his memory for some recollection of the man he was looking at. A stranger for sure, he decided. It would not be easy to forget that sharp face or that mass of snowy hair.

"Heard that head-hunter a-peppering lead at you. Figured I'd best have a look, see if you'd got yourself winged."

Shawn stepped from behind the bulge, pistol leveled. "Maybe," he said quietly. "And maybe it was you doing the shooting."

The older man drew up at Starbuck's sudden appearance. After a bit he grinned, wagged his head. "It weren't me."

"I'm supposed to just take your word for that?"

"Up to you. I was meandering along back of them hills over to the east, when I heard the shooting."

Shawn considered the reply coldly. "Be no chore for you to circle around, come at me from behind."

"No, reckon it wouldn't—if it was me. Only it sure wasn't. You meaning to use that hogleg?"

"If I have to. Step up close. Keep your hands over your head."

The old rider shrugged. Dropping the leathers of the buckskin he was leading, he raised his arms and came forward, halting when he was directly in front of Shawn.

"Name's Joe Fargo—if that counts for anything."

"It doesn't," Starbuck said flatly.

Reaching out, he lifted the man's pistol from its holster, smelled the end of the barrel. It hadn't been fired in some time. Fargo hadn't been the one to open up on him, that was sure, but he could be a partner of the man who had. Still suspicious, he thrust Fargo's weapon under his waistband and holstered his own.

Fargo relaxed. "Reckon you're satisfied now. Hell, last time I triggered that iron was more'n two weeks ago. Killed me a rattler half as big as my leg."

"I'm satisfied this wasn't the gun used—nothing more," Shawn said coldly. "Your partner still hiding out in that arroyo over there?"

The old man's brows came up. "Partner? I ain't got no partner—all by myself. Heading east for Texas. Tell you again I ain't got nothing to do with somebody trying to dry-gulch you. Mister, was it me doing that shooting, you'd be dead. I ain't missed what I shot at in forty year."

He was probably telling the truth, Shawn realized. If he was a party to the ambush, his friend would have made a move by that time. Likely it had been just as he had said. Taking the pistol from his waistband, he passed it, butt first, to the old man.

"Begging your pardon for being a mite hard-nosed about this. Just don't fancy getting shot at."

Fargo grinned, shoved his weapon into its leather. "Can't say as I can fault you none for that. Got any idea who it was?"

Starbuck shook his head. "Don't know who and I can't figure why. Thought it maybe was some stray Apache or Mexican looking to hold me up."

"Misdoubt that. They ain't apt to jump a man when they're alone. Like to run in bunches. Got themselves a cinch that way."

"That's how I looked at it. And if there'd been a bunch of them, they wouldn't have fooled around but would have hit me fast."

"Well, whoever, he sure ain't no great shakes at

shooting. Took six potshots at you and never cut a hair. Could do better with my head in a bucket. He still hanging around, you think?"

"Expect he is," Shawn said, looking off toward the hills to the west.

"Then I reckon the natural thing for us to do is chase him out. Mind telling me your name?"

"Starbuck. Shawn Starbuck."

The old puncher extended a horny hand. "Right pleased to know you, Starbuck. Done told you what I'm called."

Shawn nodded. "My pleasure. . . . Think I will cut back around see if I can get a look at that bushwhacker. No call for you to stick out your neck, however."

Joe Fargo laughed. "Kind of shooting he was doing, I don't figure a man'd be taking much of a chance. How you aiming to go about it?"

"Thought I'd move on down the arroyo a piece, circle west. He's hiding somewhere on the other side of that first line of hills."

"Be my guess, too. How'll it be for me to double back the other way, sort of ease in from that side? Maybe we can pinch him in between us."

"Ought to work," Shawn replied.

They moved out at once, Starbuck leading the sorrel down the arroyo, Fargo trailing his wiry little buckskin, heading back up the wash until he was hidden from view at the first turn.

Alone, Shawn continued for a good hundred yards until he reached a break in the wall of the cut. There, ground-reining the gelding, he climbed out through the cleft and gained the level of the flat. Glancing to his right, he saw that Fargo was already on the plain, had halted on a slight rise, his weathered features turned to the west.

Then Starbuck became aware of the quick beat of a galloping horse. He swore, realizing what it was that held the older man's attention; the bushwhacker was making a run for it. Evidently he had spotted them, had no desire to pursue his plans any further. Moving hurriedly, Shawn crossed to the nearest mound, halted, hopeful of at least getting a glimpse of the killer. He was moments too late, his efforts being rewarded with no more than a fleeting look at the rump of a horse disappearing into a wall of brush.

Taut and angry, Starbuck continued to stare at the distant mesquite and other growth into which the rider had vanished. He had lost his chance to force the bushwhacker into a face-to-face meeting, discover his identity, and learn what lay behind the attempt on his life. All he could do now was wait—and be continually on guard. A man who was so determined that he would take six shots in an effort to bring him down would certainly try again.

Coming about, he started back for the arroyo, the question of who and why again rising in his mind. He had made enemies, of course—no man moving through the frontier could expect not to—and likely among them there were a few who, nursing a deep grudge, would not be sorry to see him dead. Again he culled his memory, striving to come up with a face, a name, a remembrance of someone who might feel inclined to even a score with a bullet—and once more failed.

Reaching the arroyo, he dropped down into its depth,

moved to where the sorrel waited. Impatience was having its way with him once more, stirring up an irritability at his own failure to remember, his inability to confront the bushwhacker, have it out with him before the matter went any further. Now the moments of the future would be filled with uncertainty, and the thought would always be in his mind that somewhere in the shadows a man was looking at him down the barrel of a gun.

3

Starbuck turned to face Joe Fargo, loping up on the buckskin. "You get a look at him?" he asked as he halted beside the sorrel.

"Only the hind end of his horse when he ducked into that brush. Was a bay, or maybe a chestnut—pretty hard to tell. You see anything?"

"About the same as you."

"Sure cut out of here in a hurry. You going after him?"

Starbuck shrugged, climbed onto the sorrel. "Doesn't seem much use, considering the start he's got."

"Could try tracking—"

Shawn glanced at the sky. The day would soon be gone.

"Maybe, but likely wouldn't get far before dark."

"And maybe'd you'd walk yourself right into another ambush. Wouldn't be smart. Close up, that jasper might not miss."

Starbuck nodded in agreement. It was true also that a man trying something persistently enough eventually succeeded in the undertaking.

Joe Fargo hung a leg over his saddle horn. Removing his hat, he ran fingers through his halo of hair. "Way I see it, if he's grudging you for something and aching to square up, let him come to you. Don't do him no favors and give him the chance he's looking for by stepping into his trap. . . . You certain you ain't got no idea who he is?"

"Could be anybody far as I'm concerned."

"You sound like a man that ain't made many friends."

"Always sort of figured it was the other way around— that I didn't have many enemies."

The old puncher spat. "Well, you sure got one, and was I you, I'd keep my eyes peeled. Where you headed?"

"El Paso. Could be I'll cross the Rio and take a little jog down into Mexico."

"Then you ain't pointing for nowhere special?"

"No. I'm looking for my brother."

Fargo settled back on his saddle, his leathery features drawn into a tight study. "Starbuck," he murmured. "Don't recollect ever hearing the name before."

"Calls himself Damon Friend, too. Not sure what he looks like. Pretty much the same as me, I'm told. Little heavier."

"Still don't ring no bells."

Shawn sighed, glanced again at the sky. The eagle was gone. "There's a town the other side of those hills. You going that way?"

Fargo nodded. "Aimed to do some eating and drinking and sleeping there. You of the same notion?"

"The same," Starbuck replied, and put the sorrel into motion.

They rode in silence down the arroyo, coming finally to

a break in its east bank, where they pulled out onto higher ground. Shawn at once flung a look to the west, scouring the low hills and scraggily growth with sharp eyes. There was no one in sight.

"This here brother of yours—"

"Ben—"

"This here Ben, is it real important you find him right away?"

"Pretty much. Pa died a few years ago and things are all tied up until I find Ben and take him back so's the lawyers can straighten out the estate. Can settle down, have a place of my own then."

Fargo nodded sympathetically. "Seems every family gets into some kind of a squabble—if you don't mind my saying it."

"I don't, and there was. Between Ben and Pa. We lived on a farm in Ohio, along the Muskingum River. They had a big row one day and Ben pulled out. Was about eleven . . . no, almost twelve years ago."

Joe whistled softly. "You couldn't've been much more'n a button if you started looking for him then."

"I didn't. It was sometime later, after Pa died."

"Nobody else in the family?"

"Ben and I, we're the last. My mother died a couple of years before Ben left. Was a fine woman—a schoolteacher. I don't think there'd ever been a falling out if she'd still been around."

"Left home myself when I was a younker," Fargo said. "Weren't no more'n ten year old. Same trouble—me and my pa just couldn't get along. He was the meanest man I ever come across. Liquored up most of the time."

"Can't say that about our pa. Was strict and believed in hard work, and maybe he was a bit rough along the edges, but he was a good man. Got to know him better after we were alone." Starbuck paused, then added, "Learned plenty from him."

"About all my pa ever learned me was how to hate, and I sort of got over that once I was out on my own, meeting other folks and seeing what they were like. Had the idea when I was little that all men were like my pa, mean and no account. . . . This estate, it the farm you mentioned?"

"No, just a fair-sized chunk of cash. He had it in the will that the property was to be sold and the money put in the bank along with what he'd saved. Then it was to be split between Ben and me, after I found him and brought him back."

"So you been drifting around looking for him ever since. Reckon that ain't such a bad life at that—being able to just keep moving along, never worrying none about money."

"That's not exactly the way of it. Pa forgot to take care of that end of the deal. Means I have to find myself a job every now and then, work until I've built up a stake." Shawn paused, glanced over his shoulder. "That money laying in the bank can't be touched until I've found Ben," he finished.

Starbuck's involuntary precaution did not escape the older man's notice. A softness came into his eyes, as if he knew only too well the harsh pressure the threat of impending death at the hands of an unknown, unseen killer could lay upon a man.

"You hunting work now?" he asked, finally.

"Not especially. Got enough in my poke to last a spell. Why?"

"Thought you might be interested in riding along with me and signing up with Morgan Justice for a cattle drive."

Shawn gave it thought. There was no real reason for going to El Paso or Mexico, and on a drive he would encounter many riders, pass through several towns—all of which would afford good opportunity for making inquiries concerning Ben.

"It's something I've been doing every year for quite a spell," Fargo continued. "Just show up, sign on for the drive, then when it's over, move on. Morgan's got himself quite a spread—over in the Big Springs, Texas country."

"Seems I've heard the name."

"More'n likely. Moves out two, maybe three thousand head every spring. Always hires on a crew of drovers for the job. Has to keep his regular bunch on the ranch to look after the rest of his stock."

"Where's he send them?"

"Dodge City, since the railroad got there. We head up what some folks call the Western Trail. Runs due north and cuts across the Indian territory into Kansas. Generally takes about a month going and coming. You ever done any droving?"

Shawn nodded. "A few times. Way things've worked out for me, I've done a little of everything—including wearing a badge."

Again a gentleness filtered into the old rider's eyes. "Expect you'd be right good at that," he murmured.

22

Then, "Well, if you ain't set on going nowheres else, I'm pretty sure Morgan'll hire you on was I to ask him. Pay's good and you can be looking for your brother while you're working."

"That's what I was thinking. Happens I was in Dodge last year, but it won't hurt to drop by again. Sounds like you and Justice are old friends."

"Known him a long time, but he was the stay-put kind. Me, I sort of like to keep moving."

"I'd think maybe you'd be about ready to settle down to a good job with somebody like him."

Fargo shrugged, stared out over the broad land. "Because I'm a mite old? Hell, never have figured it that way. Age is nothing but a number folks like to go by. Means nothing. Thing that counts is how you feel—and I sure don't feel old yet."

Starbuck grinned. He could recall many men he had met who were probably around half Joe Fargo's age but were seemingly much older.

"Someday maybe I'll be ready to hang up my spurs and hunt me a rocking chair, but I don't know when. One thing I am noticing, winters seem to be a lot longer'n they used to be, and the seat of this here saddle's sure harder. I reckon I'll know, however, when the time's come."

"You figure to tie up with Justice then?"

"Probably. Got a standing offer for a job with him any-time I want. He's a fine fellow and he's got one hell of a layout. He ain't only raising longhorns but he's also fooling around with cross-breeding, using Hereford bulls that he's brung in from Kentucky. . . . There's Conejos.

You ever been there before?"

Starbuck's glance swept over the small, dusty settlement hunched in the valley below, then he turned to survey the trail behind them. The land, turned amber under the lowering sun, was silent and deserted.

"Was there once—couple of years ago."

"Got an *amigo* there that rents rooms. Can put up at his place for the night, head out for the Diamond J in the morning."

"That what Justice calls his ranch?"

"Yeh. The *J*'s for Justice, the diamond's for what he says it's worth. Makes a good brand—a diamond with a *J* inside it. . . . There's a town marshal here," he added as they rode down the steep trail that led off the mesa. "You aim to tell him about that bushwhacker?"

"No point. Nothing I can say that'll give him anything to go on."

"He was riding a dark-colored horse—"

"So are plenty of other men. Expect it's just something I'll have to handle myself."

Fargo grunted. "That's what a man usually has to do—skin his own snakes. Sort of looks like we've shook him, anyway."

"I'd like to think so," Starbuck replied. "I'm already tired of looking over my shoulder. Where's this friend of yours live?"

"Right there across the street—place called the Posada."

Shawn veered the gelding in toward the rack fronting a low, adobe brick building, noting absently as he did the half a dozen or so other structures that made up the settlement. Drawing the horse to a halt, he swung from the saddle.

A stride away Joe Fargo sighed deeply. "Like I was telling you, this danged saddle gets harder every—"

The sharp crack of a pistol, the instantaneous shattering of the Posada's glass window, cut off his words. In that same fragment of time Starbuck drew his gun and threw himself flat into the dust.

4

There was no subsequent shot. Starbuck, taut and angry, drew himself to his knees. Nearby, Joe Fargo, also prone, was swearing in a low, rumbling voice. Along the suddenly hushed street all things had come to a halt.

The bullet would have had to come from the opposite side, Shawn reasoned. He probed the structures with a sharp glance—a saloon, the general store, a café, two or three residences, a stable. Here and there the startled, strained face of some onlooker was visible through a dusty window, but he saw nothing that aroused his suspicion.

Grim, he lunged to his feet, and gun in hand, raced across the narrow street. A passageway lying between the saloon and the general store was immediately ahead of him. He ducked into it and hurried down its length until he reached the open area beyond. There was no one in sight except a woman and a child walking along a pathway leading to the main street from the houses set farther back.

Starbuck waited until they were near and then spoke.

"Ma'm, you happen to see somebody around here a bit ago?"

The woman drew up stiffly as fear filled her eyes. She stared at him for several moments, then stammered, "N—no."

He was frightening her, Shawn realized. Holstering his weapon, he pulled off his hat. "Probably was a man," he said in a quieter tone. "Could have had a gun in his hand."

"I didn't see nobody," the woman said, and grasping the child firmly, hurried on.

Starbuck continued down the alleyway, looking into each opening between the buildings carefully, checking all possible hiding places, with no results. Still taut, he returned to the street.

A dozen men were gathered around Fargo in front of the Posada, one of whom was wearing a star. Another, picking at the pieces of broken glass, in the window and dropping them to the ground, was apparently the owner of the inn. Elsewhere people were gathered in small groups outside the buildings conversing and casting glances in the direction of the inn.

Fargo, his small, dark eyes hard, looked up as Shawn approached. "Any luck?"

"None," Starbuck replied. "He must have been standing in one of the passageways, then stepped inside a door. Woman I ran into claims she saw nobody in the alley."

"Plenty of places he could've ducked into," the old puncher muttered, sweeping the buildings opposite with a glance. "Was all set and waiting for you. Must've figured we was aiming for here and circled around, come in ahead."

That seemed likely, Shawn thought. He and Fargo had taken their time riding in; the bushwhacker, moving fast, could easily have arrived well before they did.

The town lawman clucked sympathetically. "Sure is a hell of a note! You right sure you ain't got no idea who it is?"

Starbuck shrugged. "Only thing I'm sure of is that he's here now. I intend to make the rounds to see if I can spot somebody I know."

"If you do, you yell for me before you make any move," the marshal said coldly. "Don't cotton to folks taking the law into their own hands in my town."

"It would be up to him," Shawn said stiffly, and began to pull his blanket roll and saddlebags off the sorrel.

The marshal studied him thoughtfully, lips drawn into a straight, hard line. Fargo, glancing at both men, quickly broke the strained hush.

"Them two strangers that rode in this afternoon, where'd you say they was?"

The lawman's features relaxed. He shook his head. "Don't recollect saying, but that's them standing down there in front of the restaurant. . . . How long'll you be around here?"

"Pulling out in the morning—early. On our way to Morg Justice's."

Shawn had paused, looking toward the men the marshal had said were recent arrivals. One was a squat middle-aged individual in ordinary cowhand dress. The other, considerably younger, wore similar clothing except for a smaller-brimmed hat. Both were complete strangers to him.

"Been a few more passing through here on the way to Justice's," he heard the lawman say. "Fact is, them two you asked about are heading for the same place."

Fargo squinted at the pair. "That a fact? They got names?"

"Hubbard, one calls himself. Think his partner's Kent—"

"Charlie Hubbard?"

The marshal spat into the dust. "Never bothered to ask their front handles," he said indifferently. "Thing to do is see for yourself."

"Just what I'll do soon as we get bedded down," Fargo replied, and turned to the proprietor of the Posada. "Reckon you got room for me and my friend, Harry?"

"Got room for you and him and ten more," the innkeeper said morosely. "Business ain't so good. Take Number Three—end of the hall."

Harry insisted Shawn and Joe Fargo take their evening meal with him and his Mexican wife in their quarters at the rear of the hostelry. After a decent interval of idle conversation at the conclusion of the meal, they took their leave and returned to the street.

"You still figure to do what you said—look the town over for that bushwhacker?" the old rider asked as they halted at the edge of the dusty strip.

Starbuck's voice still retained an edge. "There's a chance I'll spot somebody I'll recognize."

"Expect I'd best trail along with you, then—sort of

keep an eye on your backside."

Shawn shook his head. It would be easier to move about alone. "No need. It's dark now and I'll keep pretty much out of sight. You go ahead, look up your friend Hubbard. I'll meet you later."

"Up to you," Joe said hesitantly. "Sure would hate to find you laying somewheres with a bullet smack between your shoulders."

"Not about to let that happen. Where'll you be?"

"In that saloon, if Charlie ain't changed none. Have a care, now."

"You can bet on it," Shawn said and moved off.

Keeping to the shadows in the poorly lighted street, he followed along the line of darkened store fronts, eyes thoroughly probing each passageway, each entrance and window facing him from the opposite side. He had not been exactly truthful with Joe Fargo; his plan was not designed so much to seek out the person hoping to put a bullet into him as it was to draw the man into another attempt—one that would give him an opportunity to strike back.

The odds were all in his favor that the killer would miss again, considering his previous demonstrations of marksmanship, and the powder flash of his discharged weapon, betraying his location, was all that Shawn figured he would need. He could then close in fast for an accounting.

He reached the end of the street and halted beneath the branches of a broadly spreading cottonwood. A muted rumble of voices was coming from the saloon, and somewhere in the trees surrounding the few houses scattered beyond the commercial buildings a dove mourned dole-fully. Overhead the sky glittered with stars, while a quarter moon struggled to add its pale luster to the silvery night.

The board sidewalks were deserted. Conejos was clearly a town that buttoned up early. Except for the one solitary saloon, all other businesses were closed, their somnolence lending an air of tranquillity to the hush. But it was a false impression, one of surface value only, Starbuck knew; somewhere in that peaceful stillness a man was waiting to kill him.

He walked a long five minutes and then, hand riding the butt of his forty-five, he stepped out into the open and started for the opposite side of the street. He moved leisurely, belying the tension that gripped him. The hair on the back of his neck prickled as he deliberately exposed himself. But it went for nothing. He completed the crossing without incident.

Starbuck shrugged impatiently. He had hoped to draw the killer's fire and he had failed, but he put no stock in the logical conclusion that the man must have gone; likely he was still nearby, simply biding his time.

Delaying for only a few moments, Shawn began his walk along the fronts of the structures making up the row on the west side of the lane. He passed the general store, a clothing merchant's quarters, an empty building, then came to a stop at the corner of the saloon. The lamps within the place beamed through the open doorway, casting a yellow rectangle on the sidewalk that reached partly into the street.

This could be the chance the bushwhacker was waiting

for—that moment when he could be plainly visible in good light. Starbuck braced himself, then moved directly through the strip cleaving the darkness. He grinned tautly at his own brashness—near foolhardiness, in fact, but his scheme depended upon forcing the killer's hand.

But no echoing shot crashed through the silence to challenge him. He gained the shadows on the opposite side, disappointed. The plan had failed again, and the killer certainly could have found no better opportunity. Suddenly tired, Shawn continued on to the last of the buildings, reversed himself, returned to the saloon, and entered.

There were no more than half a dozen patrons in evidence, he noted. Business was apparently as slow for the saloonkeeper as it was for Harry at the Posada. Halting at one side of the doorway, Starbuck gave the customers a close scrutinizing but recognized only Joe Fargo, who was sitting at a table near the end of the bar with the two men he had seen earlier in front of the restaurant. Responding to the old puncher's beckoning, he crossed to the table and sat down.

"This here's an old chum of mine, Charlie Hubbard," Joe said, jerking his thumb at the beefy man opposite him. "Fellow there with him is a friend of his'n, Kent."

Starbuck shook their extended hands and settled back in his chair. Hubbard was a man around the same age as Fargo; Kent was likely near his own.

Hubbard said, "Joe tells me you got somebody looking to take your scalp."

Shawn nodded humorlessly. "He's trying," and glanced

31

up at the bartender. "Rye."

"Only got bourbon."

"It'll do."

"You see anybody?" Fargo asked as the saloonkeeper moved away.

"No luck. Offered him a couple of good chances, but he didn't fall for them."

"Could be he rode on," Hubbard said. "Town sure ain't big enough for a man to hide in."

"For a fact," Fargo murmured. "Puzzlement to me why nobody seen nothing. You ask around about that?"

The bartender returned, bringing a glass and a bottle. He poured a drink for Shawn, and looked questioningly at the others. Starbuck nodded, waiting until the other men's glasses had been filled.

"Nobody around to ask. Town's locked up tight. This is the only place open."

"Marshal claimed he'd done some asking. Seen him when I first come in here. He didn't learn nothing either." Fargo paused to down his drink. Then "Is this doing changing your mind any?"

"No—"

"Fine. Charlie and Kent are headed for Justice's place, too. We can ride out in the morning together. With three of us siding you that jasper ain't apt to try throwing lead again—if he's still hanging around."

Starbuck sipped at his drink and nodded. He supposed there would be safety in numbers, but he wasn't particularly interested. Discovering who the killer was and why he sought his life was more important.

5

Near noon the next day, as they drew near the base of the Peloncillo Mountains, Starbuck shifted on his saddle and glanced back. He was riding a length behind Joe Fargo. Directly following him was Charlie Hubbard's close-mouthed friend, Kent, while Hubbard himself brought up the rear.

The arrangement made little sense to him since the bushwhacker could have singled him out in the line, but Fargo had insisted, and thus it was. From the moment they had ridden out of Conejos, after building up their trail supplies for the week-long ride ahead, he had shepherded Shawn as an old she-bear would her cub. It amused Starbuck, and he appreciated it even if he didn't particularly like it.

"Good country for renegades—Apaches and Mexes both," Hubbard called from his position in the string. "Best you all keep your eyes peeled."

Such was not news to Starbuck. He had been through the area before and had been on the alert from the time they had pulled out of the San Bernardino Valley. The trails through the Peloncillos were favored haunts for outlaw ambushes, and they would be fortunate if they made the crossing without incident.

But he reckoned they could hold their own if attacked. Four men, all well armed and experienced, except perhaps for Kent, who appeared to be fairly new to the country, would offer no easy prey to renegades; they much preferred slow-moving freight wagons and solitary parties en route west. Pack trains coming in from Mexico, often times laden with silver, were their particular objectives. They would see only a small percentage in waylaying four riders, obviously cowhands, unless their interest lay in procuring guns and ammunition.

So far it would seem they had the country to themselves. Other than a pair of coyotes and the usual number of birds, they had seen no signs of life. But as Hubbard had said, it would be wise to keep a sharp watch. To Shawn, the warning was doubly unnecessary, for not only did the rugged hills offer opportunity for banditry but they also provided ideal cover for the bushwhacker if he still pursued his purpose—and there was little doubt in Starbuck's mind concerning that.

Shortly after midday they topped out the range and began the long downgrade that would take them into the Animas Valley. With luck they would be able to camp along the base of a second string of mountains, known as the Little Hatchets, and once there, could consider themselves to be well on the way to Morg Justice's Diamond J ranch.

"Was right about here once when me and a friend got jumped," Joe Fargo said, turning half around. "Was a dozen Mexicans. Reckon they didn't want us too bad. We lit out down the mountain like the heel flies was after us, and then they started shooting. I took me a bullet in the leg first off, but it didn't hurt my gun arm none, and by the time we got to the bottom, they'd give up. Reckon we—"

Shawn did not hear the final words. Vague motion in the brush to their right drew his attention. He flung a glance at Hubbard, saw that he had noticed it also. Fargo, his back to that direction, had, of course, missed it. Kent was totally unaware of all things, being slumped in his saddle, face tipped down, dozing wearily.

"To the right," Shawn called softly. "Something in the brush."

"Seen it," Hubbard said promptly.

Fargo, again facing ahead, shifted his glance to the designated point. "Sure something. Could be your poor shooting friend. Keep your hand close to your gun."

Starbuck slid a hurried look at Kent. The man still dozed, totally unconscious of possible danger. Slowing the sorrel, Shawn dropped back until he could reach the reins of the horse Kent was riding. Grasping them, he gave a sharp jerk. The man came upright with a start.

"Good way to get killed," Starbuck said. "Keep awake. Could be running into trouble."

Kent nodded woodenly, his features bleak in the strong sunlight. "Indians?"

"Maybe," Shawn replied, and moved back into the line.

They continued on, taking care not to betray their awareness of whoever it was maintaining pace with them off trail. Apaches, Starbuck guessed. Outlaws—Mexicans or Americans—would have launched an attack instead of moving silently along at a distance. Indians always made sure of their ground before they made a move.

And it could be the bushwhacker, cruising quietly through the undergrowth, waiting for a good opportunity to single out his target. At such close range he could hardly miss again.

"Let's get out of here!" Joe Fargo yelled suddenly, and dug his spurs into the flanks of his buckskin.

Shawn reacted instantly. Roweling his own mount, he sent him spurting ahead down the trail, narrower and hemmed in by brush at that point. Behind him he heard the quick hammer of hooves as Kent and Hubbard broke their horses into a hard run.

Yells went up from the brush. Two gunshots crashed through the warm quiet, rolling across the slopes and canyons in gradually fading echoes.

" 'Paches, sure'n hell!" Hubbard shouted, and began to shoot into the dense growth.

Starbuck, bent low over the sorrel, pistol in hand, withheld his fire. He could see nothing to aim at and preferred to wait until he had a visible target. He was feeling better about it now; it wasn't the bushwhacker, and that was a relief. Even though it might be a party of renegade Indians, who presented a much more tangible danger, it strangely did not matter.

Shots were racketing steadily now, filling the air with hollow, crackling sounds. He saw a coppery shape flattened upon a pony's back cross open ground a dozen yards to his right. He fired quickly, but missed. More careful, he triggered his weapon again. The Apache slumped, spilled from his horse, and bounced limply as he struck the rock-strewn ground.

From the corner of his left eye he caught motion and twisted half about. A brave, clad only in cotton drawers and a red rag wound around his head to contain thick, black hair, was bearing down on Kent with lance poised. Starbuck fired point-blank at the brave. The bullet caught him high in the chest, knocking him backward off his horse.

"Left side, too!" Shawn yelled to make his warning heard above the pounding of the sorrel.

The trail was steep, and the animals were plunging down it at top speed, presenting almost as great a danger as the attacking Indians. But there was no slowing them. The thunder of the gunshots, the shouting braves, and the sharp grade combined to put them in a state of frenzy that would end only when they reached level ground and the Apaches had pulled off.

They were near that point. The brush was beginning to thin, and looking beyond Fargo's hunched figure, Shawn could see the green flats of the valley. An Indian appeared suddenly to the right, hammering at his pony's flanks with his heels as he bore in on the old puncher. Before Starbuck could shoot, Fargo turned, raised his pistol, and drove a bullet into the brave. The Apache yelled, flung up his arms, then slumping forward, curved off into the trees.

And then abruptly it was all over. The shooting stopped, and there was no more shouting. The steep slope was behind them, while ahead a narrow flat covered with grass and scattered clumps of brush stretched out toward the mountains to the east.

But Joe Fargo did not pull in until they had put a long mile between the foot of the trail and themselves. He was taking no chances on a second attack. They had been lucky, and he was not a man to press good fortune.

Finally slowing, he waited for the rest to catch up scrutinizing each of them as they drew together.

"Anybody get hisself hurt?"

Starbuck shook his head and turned to the others. Kent had apparently escaped injury. Charlie Hubbard held up an arm to show a bloody streak across his wrist.

"Reckon you could say I been grooved." He grinned. "How many of them devils you figure was out there?"

"Six, maybe eight. We winged about half of them."

"Expect that was what took all the sand out of them. Must've been our guns they was after."

Shawn felt Kent's eyes pressing him and he nodded. "Glad you made it all right. First time you ever run up against Indians?"

The young man bobbed his head. "First time. I—I own you some thanks. That one—"

"Forget it. You'd've done the same for me."

"That jaybird liked to fooled us all!" Hubbard said. "Never seen him at all until Starbuck nailed him square in the brisket. We camping in the Hatchets?"

Joe Fargo looked off toward the distant hills, blue-gray in the sunlight. "Be my choice if it's jake with the rest of you. It'll be smart to get plenty far from the Peloncillos. Don't think them redskins'll make another try, but there just ain't no figuring them. They could."

"What I been mulling, too," Hubbard said. He swung his eyes to Kent. "Can say you been blooded now, boy. Had your first taste of shooting and being shot back at."

The bleakness had not left Kent's features. He stirred slightly. "Are we likely to run into more of them?"

Fargo scrubbed at his jaw. "Ain't no saying for sure that we won't. Got the Mescalero country to go through yet, but they've been peaceable lately, I hear."

"If you've got your belly full of this kind of living," Hubbard said sympathetically, "why, we'll be coming to Las Cruces in a couple of days. Won't nobody fault you was you to drop off there. It's a pretty nice little town."

Kent shook his head. "No, I'll stick."

"Fair enough," Fargo said, and looked again toward the range of mountains in the distance. "Well, let's move out. We still got a far piece to go."

Late in the afternoon of the eighth day out of Conejos they rode into the Diamond J. Fargo and Charlie Hubbard, both frequent if sporadic employees of Morgan Justice, headed immediately for the big brick house set on white fieldstones at the foot of a low hill. Trees, shrubbery, and brightly colored flowers grew in profusion.

As they drew up to the whitewashed hitchrack that fronted the structure, Fargo cupped a hand to his mouth and shouted, "Hey, Morg—we're here!"

Moments later, a large, paunchy, red-faced man—looking more the successful politician than a rancher except for the fancifully tooled, hand-made boots he wore outside the pegged legs of his trousers—pushed through the screen door and stepped out onto the veranda. Grinning broadly, he came down the steps, hand extended.

"Joe, you old bastard! Knew you'd be back!"

He swung to Hubbard. "Same goes for you, old hoss. I sure am glad to see the both of you!" He paused, sizing up Shawn and Kent with a narrow glance. "Who're these here fellows? You both got so old and stove-in you had to have a swamper helping you on and off your horses?"

"Not yet," Fargo answered. "Me and Charlie just figured you'd be needing some good help, so we brung them along. Morg, shake hands there with Starbuck and Kent."

The rancher moved to Shawn, and then to the other rider, taking their hands in a brief, firm grip. "I'm welcoming you both, and if Joe and Charlie lag for you, then you're fine with me."

"How's the missus?" Fargo asked, looking toward the house.

"Mighty fine. She'll sure be pleased to hear you've showed up. Step down and we'll go inside."

"Not till I do some washing off and duds-changing first. Ain't no sheep dog ever smelled bad as I do right now. . . . Tom Zook still doing your ramrodding?"

"Still my number-one man. Reckon you'll find him down at the bunkhouse."

Fargo bobbed his head. "Best we get over there and let him know we've come."

"Do that," Justice said heartily, "then get yourself back up here so's you can take supper with me and Jenny. We'll be waiting."

"I'll be there, come time," the old puncher said, and swinging away from the rack cut across the cleanly swept hardpack for a cluster of low-roofed buildings a hundred yards or so away.

"Old Morg never changes," Hubbard said, shaking his head admiringly.

"Ain't got no reason to. Plenty of money, good ranch

40

with more cattle than a goose's got feathers—and a good woman for a wife."

Hubbard cast a side glance at his friend. "For a fact," he said, and abruptly grinned. "Say, ain't that Will Vance and Roy Chesson there by the horse corral?"

"By hell it is!" Fargo shouted. "Never figured they'd make another drive. Hey, Roy—Will!"

The two men crossing the area that lay between the crew's quarters and the pole-fenced enclosure where the riding stock was kept halted, stared. Suddenly both broke into a shambling run, yelling and smiling broadly as they waved their arms in greeting. The noise brought three other riders out of the bunkhouse, and by the time Shawn and the others had reached the rack at the side of the structure, all were there waiting.

There was a general round of greetings and then Chesson stepped up to Fargo. "Sure glad to see you," he said, and making a pretense of helping Joe off his horse, added, "Ain't you a mite old to be forking a saddle and setting out to nurse cows?"

"I ain't dead yet so I ain't too old," Fargo retorted, and pushed the men away with his foot.

"Who else's showed up?" Hubbard asked, glancing around.

"Pretty near the same bunch." Vance answered. "Who you got with you?"

"Big one there's named Starbuck. He's sort of hunting his brother while he does his droving. Curly-haired one calls hisself Kent. You all step up and name yourself."

Chesson and Will Vance crossed to Shawn and Kent and introduced themselves. They were followed by four others—Troy Dakan, Amos Green, Sim Roberson, and a gangling oldster who gave only the name, Eli. The introductions were done with the stiff solemnity of men accustomed to working among friends and seldom called upon to meet strangers.

"Tom hereabouts close?" Fargo asked, hanging his blanket roll and saddlebags upon a shoulder.

"Close enough," a voice called from the doorway of the bunkhouse.

Starbuck wheeled with the others. The foreman was a lean, rawhide sort of man with dark eyes, hair, and mustache, and skin that looked like old leather. There was a toughness to him, and the smile he produced was little more than a crack in his tight-set lips.

"You're coming in late. Was about to give up on the both of you. Who's that siding you?"

"Couple friends of ours," Fargo said, and introduced Shawn and Kent. "Reckon you've got room for them."

It was more a statement of completed fact, not a question. Zook nodded. "Expect I have. They know what droving's all about?"

"Starbuck's been around plenty. Kent there'll get by."

The foreman frowned. "You know Morg's rule—"

"He'll do, I'll see to that," Hubbard said. "You got a full crew yet?"

"Have now."

"When you aim to move out?"

"Day after tomorrow."

"How many head we driving?"

"Three thousand this year."

"Whoo—ee! Dodge City again?"

Zook nodded. "Same town, same trail, same buyer." He paused as four more punchers came around the corner of the bunkhouse. "Here's the rest of the boys. Don't think you know them."

Fargo looked them over. "No, reckon we don't," he said bluntly.

Zook waited until the quartet had halted at the edge of the porch. Laying a hand on the shoulder of the nearest, he said, "This here's Cass Walton. One next to him is Gus Yeager. Then there's Gabe and Cal Ligon. They're from over San Antone way. Boys, you've heard tell of Joe Fargo. That's him there by the buckskin. Other old coot's Charlie Hubbard. Their friends are called Starbuck and Kent—he's the one with the sheepherder hat."

Once more there was a round of hand-shaking, followed by several minutes of general conversation. Starbuck, cool and remote as he usually was at such times, considered the men quietly. Later he would seek them out one by one, ask about Ben. Evidently all were old hands on the trail, and likely had spent most of their lives drifting about. It was possible that one among them could have encountered his brother and would be able to furnish him with some helpful information. Also, there was Morgan Justice's regular crew; it would be wise to talk with them too. Taking up his gear, he turned with the others toward the bunkhouse entrance. Will Vance fell in beside him.

"Joe was telling me you had yourself a bit of excitement coming over."

Shawn brushed at the sweat on his face with a free hand. "Apaches. Took a fancy to our guns, we figure."

"I'm meaning that bushwhacker that keeps taking pot-shots at you."

"Oh, yeh. Been lucky so far. I'm hoping he'll keep on missing until I can find out who he is."

"Sure does seem set on nailing you. Reckon he trailed you to here?"

"Possible."

Vance swore quietly. "Well, I'll be doing some hoping, too—that he didn't. When we get on the trail with a herd as big as we're taking, it sure won't be no place for some crazy galoot with a itchy trigger finger. We'll be having our hands full as it is."

Shawn gave that thought. "Hadn't thought of it, but I expect it could mean trouble. Might be best I back out."

"Could be," Vance said. "I been on hoodooed drives before and it ain't no picnic."

Starbuck halted on the porch, turned, looked for Tom Zook. As well let the foreman know his situation now, not wait until later when leaving would cause him to go short-handed. Zook was standing off to one side in conversation with Joe Fargo, his dark features drawn into a frown.

"Something wrong?" Kent asked. He had been walking behind Starbuck.

Starbuck passed his gear to the rider. "Go on inside, pick us a couple of bunks—near a window. There's a little talking I'd best do with that foreman before I settle in."

Kent accepted Shawn's saddlebags and blanket, crowded past him, and entered the rambling structure. Starbuck, nodding to Vance, stepped off the porch and crossed to Zook and Fargo. The Diamond J ramrod looked up as he approached.

"Joe's been telling me about you," he said.

"What I came here for. Figure you ought to know."

Zook pushed back his hat. "Obliged to you for that. Think he's followed you?"

"No way of knowing. We kept a sharp lookout on our back trail, but never saw anybody. There was plenty of chances for him to try again, had he been around."

"Just what I told Tom," Fargo said. "I figure we lost him somewheres on the yonder side of the Peloncillos. One thing sure, we got them Apaches between us and him."

"Could be they got him," Zook said. "Can't see as it makes any difference. I'm willing if you are. Joe says you're a good one to ride the river with, and I can't recollect when he was wrong last."

"Appreciate that, but if you've got any doubts I'll quit now. Don't want to be the cause of any trouble."

The foreman snorted. "Hell, there's three weeks of days and night between here and Dodge, and a man can't sidestep trouble along the way no matter how hard he tries! Besides, we ain't greenhorns, none of us, unless you count that friend of Hubbard's. If that jasper shows up looking for you, I reckon we can handle anything he can start."

Shawn smiled. "Not bothered much about myself. Figure I can look after my own hide—it's that I don't want to be a hoodoo—"

"Hoodoo!" Joe Fargo exploded. "You been talking to Will Vance?"

"We passed some words about—"

"Knowed it! Never should've told him about you! He's worse'n one of them gypsies about things like that. He put that notion in your head to quit?"

"Figured it might cause trouble."

"Well, you just forget it," Zook said. "Will Vance ain't running things around here, and if he's all spooked up about it, then he can do the quitting."

Fargo heaved a deep sigh. "Proud to hear you say that, Tom. Well, I best be getting a move on. Boss is expecting me for supper, and I need cleaning up. Shawn, you fix yourself in the bunkhouse. The boys will show you where the eating's done. I'll see you later on."

Fargo moved off at his peculiar mincing gait. Zook watched him for a bit, and wagged his head. "One hell of a man that Joe," he said. "Can set a saddle all day and half the night and still be ready to ride again the next morning. Wish't I could say the same for myself."

Reaching up, he straightened his hat. "You go on, forget what Vance said, fix yourself a bed. We'll be eating in about a hour. . . . Got a few things I got to do first."

The foreman smiled briefly, then wheeled away. Shawn turned and retraced his steps to the bunkhouse. All but Will Vance had disappeared into its shadowy interior when he reached the porch. The older man was leaning against a roof support, his face intent.

"You tell him?"

"Didn't need to. Joe had already given him the story."

"What'd he say?"

"I offered to quit. He said to forget it."

Vance swore deeply. "Tom's making a fool mistake," he said in a low voice. "Ain't meaning nothing personal, but you're going to saddle us with a heap of trouble. I'm betting there won't be half of us gets back from this drive alive."

7

Joe Fargo rose from the deep-cushioned, rawhide chair in which he was sitting, and forcing a smile, nodded first to Morgan Justice and then to Jenny.

"Been a powerful long day, and my bones are aching to call it quits. Reckon I'd best turn in."

The rancher got to his feet hurriedly. "Now there ain't no call for you to be going far as I'm concerned," he said. "Me and the wife never do get to bed sooner than ten, maybe eleven o'clock."

"Was a mighty fine meal," Fargo continued, turning his glance to the woman. "But I always said you was the best cook in the county."

He looked away, regretting the words instantly, realizing they served not as a compliment as he had intended, but as a raking open of old scars.

"Thank you, Joe," she said quietly.

Fargo pivoted on his heel, and trailed by the rancher, moved toward the door at the far end of the big, well-furnished room. What Morgan Justice had built for a home was as near a mansion as a man could find in the deep Texas country—and a far cry from the humble dwellings he had been able to provide when Jenny was his.

"Tom says we're pulling out in a couple of days,"

Fargo said, hesitating in the doorway. "Was I not to see you again before that, I will when I get back."

"Hell, you'll see me all right!" Justice declared, slapping him on the back. "I'll be there when you head out with my stock. Besides, I'll be in the yard now and then."

Joe Fargo was looking beyond the rancher at Jenny. Her hair had become a bit grayer, he noted, and the small crinkles at the corners of her eyes and around her lips had deepened since last year. But there was still that patient gentleness about her that he had once come to hate. Now he saw it in a different light—as a sort of laudable attribute. Why does a man have to learn things the hard way sometimes?

"Then I reckon we'll be talking again," he murmured and stepped out onto the wide veranda. "Good night."

"Same to you, partner!" Justice boomed.

If Jenny had responded to his leave-taking, it went unheard. As in all other ways she had become so completely submerged in Morg's big, bluff personality that she was little more than a wispy shadow. But that was what Jenny had wanted, and if, after it was all over, she had any regrets, she never permitted them to become apparent.

Descending the steps, he paused as he heard the door click shut—a solid, final sound that closed him out of a world partly of his own making, and glanced toward the bunkhouse.

The evening was warm and pleasant. Most of the hands not riding night herd were lounging on the porch shooting the bull and telling jokes while they took their ease. Someone had built a small fire on the hardpack, not so much for warmth as for the friendly cheer it provided, and three or four of the punchers were sprawled nearby, the tips of their cigarettes like round, red eyes in the half dark.

Scanning the group, he located Starbuck. A smile parted his lips. A lot like me fifty years ago, he thought to himself, and he looks much like James would, he noted bitterly. Far too much; if Jenny saw him she would feel a wrench that would near tear her in two.

James would be a bit older than Shawn, if he had still been alive, but he had that same straight way of standing and walking—like he was daring the world to take him on—and that same dark hair that sort of curled around his ears, and sharp eyes that seemed to cut right through a man. There was no way of knowing, of course, how James would have turned out had he lived, but it was nice to think he would have been like Starbuck.

Fargo, far from being tired as he had complained earlier, moved off slowly along a row of lilacs that formed a hedge separating the yard from the house. Undoubtedly they had been planted by Jenny, for they had always been one of her favorite flowers. Unnoticed by the men, he circled around to the corrals, and there, hunkering down on his heels, he dug into his shirt pocket for the makings of a cigarette and rolled himself one.

Shielding a match with a cupped hand, he fired it with a thumbnail, sucked the slim, brown cylinder into life, and settled back. Things hadn't turned out so bad after all, he guessed; Jenny had ended up with what she wanted—or thought she wanted—and he was content. That was all that mattered, he supposed, being content. A man always had to compromise with life somewhere along the line.

But there were times when he couldn't help wondering how it would have been if they hadn't had James. Would Jenny have then been content with their way of life, or would she have found some other reason for hating the star he wore and the job he was called upon to uphold?

The job had been the real cause of the break up; he knew that now, just as he'd known it then. A deputy U.S. marshal in Nebraska, at a time when things were rough and plenty wild, he had found himself on the move almost continually. Such absences placed the chore of raising their son on Jenny's shoulders—a task never easy in any frontier town that could offer little in the way of civilized living.

As the years passed she had become increasingly dissatisfied with their lot, and the infrequent days when he was home were filled with a tense aura of hostility and frustration that kept them both living on the edge of a volcano, the only cure for which, according to Jenny, was resigning his commission and leading the normal life enjoyed by other men.

But the star was his life, and strangely, had cost James his. On a blustery night during one of his occasional layovers, a knock had sounded on the door. James, barely out of his teens, rose to answer and took a shotgun blast squarely in the chest from an escaped, vengeance-minded killer.

Everything had ended there—the boy's life, their marriage, and his devotion to the star he wore. Jenny had turned from him spiritually as well as legally, soon wedding their close friend Morgan Justice, and he had taken to the trail, forsaking all the old ties.

Years later he had wandered into Texas and discovered that Justice, who had been a successful merchant back in Nebraska, had sold out his interests, moved, and had gone into the cattle-raising business, and was considered the top rancher in his part of the country.

Curiosity, and perhaps a genuine need to see Jenny again, had prompted his paying them a call. He had been both pleased and relieved to find the reunion evoked only a little hurt—a pain that neither lessened nor increased, but hung stationary as does a cloud trapped in a box canyon.

He supposed he should stop coming to the Diamond J, that he should never have visited and later hired out to Morg in the first place; but somehow, like the Mexican sect of flagellants known as the *penitentes,* who gather annually to chastise themselves for past misdeeds, such visits seemed to purge and ease the guilt that forever reminded him of how things might have been had he listened to Jenny.

The cigarette was dead between his lips. He reached up, took it between thumb and forefinger, and flipped it off into the night. Most of the riders still lounged in front of the bunkhouse, and rising, he angled across the sun-baked yard toward them. The voice of Will Vance, faintly derisive, came to him.

"That there high-toned buckle you're wearing, it mean you're some kind of a champion fighter?"

Will was speaking to Starbuck. Fargo had also noticed the belt when they first met and had silently admired the oblong piece of scrolled silver with the ivory figure of a boxer set into it.

"Belonged to my pa," Shawn replied in his low, easy manner. "Never was a champion, but I expect he could have been had he wanted. Liked farming better, I guess."

"How about you? He learn you how to do your fighting that la-de-da way?"

Starbuck's reply was slow in coming. "Gave my brother and me both a few lessons."

Fargo halted at the comer of the bunkhouse. The other punchers were quiet, intent, seemingly caught up by the words passing between the two men. Trouble. . . . He recognized it at once in Vance's snide tone, in the taut, controlled manner in which Shawn answered.

"Ain't never yet seen one of you fancy-Dans that could stand up to a real man. You ever lick anybody?"

"Not counting gals," a voice near the dwindling fire added.

There were a few snickers. Starbuck shrugged. "Had no problem looking after myself so far."

"That mean you're willing to stand up and do some fighting right here and now?" Vance pressed in a hurried way.

"No reason—"

The older man laughed, glanced around. "No reason except that maybe you're plain scared to meet a honest-to-God fighter like Gabe there."

Anger stirred Fargo. Will Vance knew better than to stir up trouble among the crew. His eyes sought out Gabe. He was one of the new ones—a big, burly redhead with no neck and the shoulders of a bull.

"Sure," someone on the porch chimed in. "How about us having a little show—the fancy-Dan against Gabe. Ought to be right interesting."

Will Vance, squatting on his heels, flipped a twig at the redhead. "What say, Gabe? You willing to show Starbuck how a man's supposed to do his fighting?"

The husky puncher stirred, sat up. "I'm willing. Reckon it's up to him."

Vance swung his sly eyes to Starbuck. "You hear that? You game?"

"I ain't," Joe Fargo snapped, stepping out of the shadows. "There ain't going to be no scrapping now or any other time. What the hell's eating you?" he added, facing Vance. "You know goddam well what'd happen if them boys started mixing it up!"

"Now, wait just a—"

"Tom Zook'd be out here in thirty seconds frothing at the mouth. You know he don't stand for no fighting among the crew. He'd fire both of these boys quick as he seen what was going on. You wanting him to run them off, that it?"

Vance picked up another twig and tossed it into the fire. "Was only aiming to have a little fun."

"Fun! You call getting them two throwed off the place fun?" Fargo paused, wagging his head. "Can't figure you, Will. You plain know better. What's got into you?"

Vance rose. "Nothing much," he said, and swinging about, started for the bunkhouse door. "I'm turning in."

Thoughtful, Joe Fargo watched him disappear into the building. He had been acquainted with Vance for several years, recognized the fact that the man possessed certain peculiarities, but he had never seen him pull a stunt like this. Tom Zook was known to be a stickler when it came to crew behavior, and was even stricter with his drovers, since hard feelings and ill will could be a source of costly trouble during a long, monotonous trail drive. It was as if Vance actually wanted to see Gabe and Starbuck fired; or was it only Starbuck he was after? Fargo's eyes narrowed as he gave that consideration.

"Reckon we all best be crawling into our blankets," Roy Chesson said, getting to his feet. "Few more days and we'll be wishing we had the chance."

The sprawling men stirred and began to head for their beds. Starbuck passed close by, his strong features impassive. Fargo dropped in behind him, a wistfulness tugging at his insides. It would have made him proud if James had lived to grow up and be like Shawn.

Tom Zook, his face glistening with sweat in the driving sunlight, leaned forward in the saddle and considered the men gathered before him. He made a slight gesture at the dark, wiry Mexican beside him.

"For them of you that's new around here, this is Manny, the wrangler. He don't mind being called a Mex if you don't make it sound like a cuss word."

The foreman pointed then to a bearded, white-haired oldster in plaid shirt and faded bib overalls who was leaning against the corral. "That gent there's Arkansas. He'll be doing the cooking and the doctoring. Can pull teeth, if it becomes needful."

"Yeh, but can he cook?" a voice from among the drovers called.

"Ain't nobody ever starved yet," Zook replied humorlessly. "Now about the paying. Mr. Justice lays out sixty dollars for the drive. Know that's more'n most other ranchers hereabouts pay, but he expects more than other ranchers. He wants losses kept rock bottom, same as he wants his stock kept in good shape and in Dodge on time.

"Means you're going to be working mighty damned hard—right up to the time when we close the gate in the last loading pen. You'll get your money then, and you'll be free to bust loose, blow the roof off the out house all you please. Now, there any questions?"

"When we moving out?"

"This afternoon."

A mutter of surprise ran through the crowd. Word had been that the drive would begin the next day. Zook was calling for an earlier start. It meant nothing to the drovers except that it was a change, and that kind of thing was grounds for objection.

"Thought you said tomorrow!"

"I did, but the herd's ready—and you're all here and just setting around. Might as well get going. Cattle'll get trail broke just that much sooner."

"Won't get far in just an afternoon," Yeager, who was standing with Shawn and Kent, observed sourly, and then added, "hell, we had us a card game all lined up for tonight."

"Pulling out ahead of time'll probably save you some money," the foreman said drily. "Anybody else wanting to speak up? No? All right, I take it we're all set. Quick as you've done your eating, pack up and head out to the *Brecha*—due east of here about three mile. The gather's there. Now, don't take too long with your vittles. We're moving out at two o'clock sharp. Any man that ain't there ready to ride is looking for a new job."

Starbuck grinned. He liked Tom Zook's way of doing a job. He told a man straight out the way things were to be and left no doubt that he meant every word he spoke.

"Seems sort of foolish to me to be starting so late," Kent said irritably.

"Wants to get the herd strung out," Starbuck replied. "Don't think he expects to cover much ground before dark. You ready to go?"

"What's to get ready? Nothing special about driving a bunch of cattle to market—except it takes a while longer."

Shawn looked more closely at the man and frowned. "This your first drive?"

Kent shrugged. "I've been on the trail before."

He was avoiding the truth—bluffing. Starbuck smiled. There had been times after he'd begun the search for Ben when he'd pulled the same thing. Desperate for cash, he had often professed experience in order to get work. He, perhaps, had been a bit more fortunate, however. Growing up on a farm, he possessed a basic knowledge of cattle and horses; Kent undoubtedly came from a city.

Shawn glanced at Yeager, still nearby, hoping he had not overheard. Many seasoned drovers had an aversion that amounted almost to refusal when it came to making a drive with a greenhorn. If word should get around . . . but Yeager apparently had not been listening.

"Horse of mine's not in too good condition," Kent said, his manner relenting somewhat. "Not sure he—"

Shawn touched him on the arm, then turned away and moved toward the adjacent corral where their horses were. Yeager did not follow.

"You won't have to worry about what you ride. Took a look at the *remuda* early this morning."

"Remuda?" Kent echoed.

Again Starbuck stared at the man. "The extra horses they bring along. We'll be hard on them and have to change pretty often."

"I know," Kent murmured. "Just didn't recognize that word. Mexican, isn't it?"

Shawn nodded. He was not being fooled; Kent didn't even know about such necessary things as spare mounts for the drovers. He was going to need a lot of help holding up his end on the drive, and his pride was going to make accepting that help difficult. But he deserved his chance, and Starbuck guessed he could overlook the man's resentment.

Entering the corral, he roped the sorrel, brought him outside to the rack, and began a careful check of the gelding for any unnoticed injuries or loose shoes. Satisfied that all was well, he saddled and bridled the big horse, after which he fell to examining his gear to make certain it, too, was in good condition.

"Was wondering where you'd got to."

At Joe Fargo's voice Shawn turned and grinned. "Taking Zook at his word. Aim to be on the spot and ready to ride just like he said."

The old puncher bobbed his head. "Good idea—and

sure something them others best be doing. Tom don't chaw his tobacco twice. I see Charlie's friend's right busy at it, too."

Starbuck followed Fargo's line of gaze. Kent had gotten his white-stockinged bay from the pen and was readying him, also.

"Seen some handier fellows with leather in my time," the older man said drily.

"Don't think he's been around ranching long. He won't admit it, but he'll be needing some help."

"Figured that when I first sized him up. But I ain't one of them, howsomever, that's against giving a man his chance."

"I feel the same. Always be obliged to the folks who gave me mine. What about Zook? Surprised he hasn't spotted it."

"He will, once we get moving. Right now he's taking Charlie Hubbard's word for him, same as he took my vouching for you. Be up to Charlie to smooth Tom's feathers." Fargo hooked a leg over the hitchrack and stroked his mustache. "Meant to ask earlier—you and Will Vance have words about something?"

"He figures me being on the drive will cause trouble—that bushwhacker. Wanted me to back out."

"Oh, that. Did you tell him you'd talked to Tom about it?"

Shawn nodded. "Told him he knew and that he said it was all right."

"But it didn't swallow down too good?"

"Not much. Thinks Zook is making a big mistake."

Fargo continued to smooth his mustache. "See now

why he was trying to start a ruckus last night. He was hoping to get you fired."

"Came close to it. I'd have taken on Gabe if you hadn't horned in. Man can listen to just so much talk like—"

"Well, by dang, you keep on listening to it!" Fargo snapped. "Don't want you walking into no traps like that!"

Shawn stared at the older man, startled by his vehemence. It was a little like being around Hiram Starbuck again—taking his orders, listening to his advice.

Joe Fargo grinned self-consciously, then spat. "Don't mean to be butting in or nothing like that," he said. "Reckon you're man enough to take care of yourself, but that Will Vance makes me plumb sore. There's a lot of drovers that're real spooky about a drive—always talking hoodoo and jinx, and stuff like that—"

"Superstitious—"

"Yeh, that's it. Will's one of the worst, and some of them others are about as bad, so don't you let none of them euchre you into a tight spot. But if you do come up needing some help, just figure on me being handy. Hear?"

"Obliged to you," Shawn said. "You can figure on me, too."

Fargo slapped his palms together. "Fine! We'll do our chumming together, and when we get to Dodge I know a few folks that I aim to talk to about your brother. Just could be I can fix you up with a way to get in touch with him."

"A way?" Starbuck repeated.

"Sure—a kind of a mail service thing. Used it myself once when I was moving around a lot. Ain't sure it's still working, but we'll find out when we get there. Was a scheme where folks pass the word along to other folks down the line."

Shawn felt his hopes rise. Such an idea had never occurred to him—at least not as an organized program. He had dropped word here and there many times, realizing that his descriptions were probably forgotten a few hours after he had ridden on.

"Sounds good."

"Just might do the trick for you," Fargo said, squaring himself on his booted feet. "Well, got a little personal business to take care of. See you later at the *Brecha.*"

Shawn nodded, watching the older man move off. It could be that his visit to Dodge City this time would pay off insofar as Ben was concerned—assuming he got there. Eyes narrowing, he pondered that sobering, second thought; had he shaken the bushwhacker or was the killer still around, awaiting his chance?

Joe Fargo swung clear of the Justice house and hurried on toward the little grove above it where Jenny would be waiting. He had expected to hear from her, knowing well that once she glimpsed Shawn Starbuck old memories would return and she would feel the need to talk with him again. He didn't much like the idea of sneaking around Morg Justice's back to effect a meeting, however, and the whole thing made him a bit edgy and impatient.

He found Jenny sitting on a log set well back among the trees. She rose at his approach, features alight and eyes glowing in a way that took him swiftly back over the years.

"Oh, Joe—that new man, Starbuck! Have you noticed how much he looks like James?"

Fargo nodded. "I've noticed. How'd you know his name?"

"I asked Tom. . . . It's almost the same as having our son around again. Is he like him in other ways?"

"Little hard for me to answer that. Me and James never did get much acquainted. But I like to think so. Shawn's a fine boy."

"Shawn . . . Shawn Starbuck." Jenny murmured the words softly. "It's a pretty name. Is he your friend?"

"Sort've taken a fancy to him, and him to me, I reckon. Aim to help him find his brother so's he can settle down like he wants. . . . Kind of risky, you sending for me to meet you here like this. Be a mite hard to explain to Morg."

"I know, but I couldn't help it. Seeing Shawn, and him reminding me so much of James—I just had to talk to you. Joe, do you ever think much of the old days? Of when we were together, I mean."

He watched her resume her place on the log, and then pulling off his hat, sat down beside her.

"Little hard not to. Things you never forget."

"I know that—only too well. Each time I remember it cuts a little deeper."

He glanced at her in surprise. "You saying you're sorry we busted up?"

Jenny was staring off into the trees, her eyes misty and soft. "I suppose I am. I've thought that often enough, but never had the courage to admit it even to myself. I guess it was seeing that boy—can you ever forgive me, Joe?"

Fargo stirred wearily. "It's me that has to be forgiven. I ought've listened to you, and not put my job ahead of living. Little late to be talking about it, howsomever."

"It'll never be too late—not for us."

Again he looked up at her in surprise. "You thinking we ought to go back together?"

"Would you want to?"

"Maybe, but it just ain't in the cards. Me, I got nothing now to give you. Just another saddlebum riding the trails. Morg's rich. You can have anything you want."

"Anything," she repeated in an empty voice, "but the way things used to be. You could settle down, Joe, find a job. I'd be happy with whatever you did."

"Mite late for that, too. Ain't as young as I once was."

"You could get a job somewhere as a ranch hand. You do harder work than that now—driving cattle."

Abruptly she turned eagerly to him. "You said something about helping Shawn find a brother so he could have a place of his own. Maybe, if you do, you could go to work for him!"

Joe Fargo considered that in silence. Then, "Just might work out. . . . It'd be sort of nice being around him all the time—like having a son again."

Her question came all in a breath. "Do you think there's a chance?"

He reached over, laying his hand upon hers as he sought to calm the excitement gripping her. "Can do some looking into it. You sure it's what you want?"

She nodded hurriedly, and then the gladness faded. "Morgan, he'd never—"

"Morg'll be my chore. You let me do the talking to

him," he said, rising. "And that'll come if things work out for Starbuck, and after we get back from Dodge."

Jenny was on her feet instantly and clinging tightly to him. "Oh, Joe—all those years gone! I'm so sorry—"

"Fault me, too," he said huskily. "Reckon we both made our mistakes, but the good Lord willing, maybe we can make up for them."

Jenny pulled back, carefully hiding her face from him. He patted her gently on the shoulder.

"Now, you get a hold of yourself and don't say nothing to nobody. Just leave everything up to me. Hear?"

"I hear," she murmured.

Wheeling, he started back down the path, then paused. Looking around he touched the brim of his hat with a forefinger. "So long, my lady," he said, and continued on. It had been a long time since he'd used that farewell.

Starbuck glanced to the sky—a clean, hot blue except for a few clouds piling up in the far southeast. It was the second day out of the *Brecha* and the cattle were still fractious and not trailing as they should.

"When do we come to water?" he asked.

Joe Fargo, riding flank with him, shook his head. "Tomorrow, about noon—maybe. Sure an ornery bunch of critters!"

Shawn spurred off to his left to intercept a small jag of steers breaking away from the main herd, determined to strike out on their own. He was riding a chunky little gray gelding, the sorrel getting a bit of rest after some earlier hard use.

The steers swung into a different direction and broke into a run as the gray cut across in front of them. The gelding, an old hand at this, veered sharply with them, matching them stride for stride as they raced along. The contest continued for a short distance, and then the steers, giving up, rejoined the herd.

"Been like that ever since we moved out," Fargo said as Starbuck dropped the gray back into place. "Man'd think we was driving hogs. Just won't stay bunched."

"Going to get worse if we don't hit water before tomorrow."

"Know that, and the worst of it is, that there creek we're figuring on could be dry or maybe so low it won't count for nothing."

Shawn brushed at the sweat and dust on his face. "Why'd Zook pick this trail? It the only one?"

"It's the shortest."

"But with no water—"

"Usually ain't the way of it. Always been a few sinks holding enough rainwater to keep the dang critters happy. This year they all been dry. Tom says there just ain't been no spring rains like there generally is."

Starbuck shifted on his saddle, looking out over the broad, moving blanket of colored hides and flashing horns. The hovering dust was so thick he could not see the opposite side of the herd; nearby riders were vague, ghostly shapes in the haze.

"We'd all better hope that creek's not dry," he said grimly. "Going to be hell holding them down as it is."

"For sure," the old puncher replied, and spurred on

ahead, doubled rope swinging from his hand as another bunch of steers split off from the herd.

The hours wore on, hot, filled with choking dust, the bawling of the fretful cattle, and the shouts of sweating drovers struggling to keep them in a single pack. Late in the afternoon Tom Zook rode by, his lean face streaked with dirt, weariness showing in his reddened eyes.

"Having much trouble?"

"No more than anybody else," Shawn answered.

"Then I reckon you're having plenty. Worst bunch of flea-bit *mulas* I've ever seen. Something in the air spooking them."

"When we get to water they'll likely settle down."

Zook rubbed at the back of his neck. "It'll help, that's for damn sure, but there's something more'n that. They're jumpy and it ain't wearing off like it ought."

"Could be that storm coming. Clouds to the south and east."

"Means nothing. Been doing that for a month. Clouds show up, then just hang there and the air gets a sort of dry, crackly feeling—and the rain never comes. You seen anything of that friend of yours, Kent?"

"Not since morning. Was riding point then, him and Hubbard and a couple others. Probably still there. He do something wrong?"

"No, fact is he's doing fine. Course Charlie's nursing him along. Them two figured they'd pulled the wool over my eyes, thinking that I didn't spot him for a greenhorn. Seen it first off, but I was short one man and Hubbard was all fired up to take him by the hand so I went along with it. Where's Joe?"

"On up a ways."

Zook hawked, spat, and sleeved the dust from his eyes. "Good. Want to talk to him. Aim to pull up in about five miles. Sort of a valley. Usually got a fair-sized water hole, but I expect it'll be dry like all the rest. *Adios*."

Shawn watched the Diamond J foreman fade into the drifting dust. There was something in what he'd said about the cattle's nervousness. Often he'd heard old-time drovers speak of how a herd could sense the approach of a bad storm, even though there was no visible evidence. He glanced again to the sky. The clouds were still there, just hanging motionless as Tom Zook had stated. That they would produce rain any time in the near future seemed a remote possibility.

It was near dark when they reached the swale Zook had mentioned, and as he had predicted, the water hole had dried up. Only the fact that there was a good stand of grass available kept the cattle from giving the punchers more trouble than they did.

Arkansas was there ahead of them, his shuttler pulled up under a chinaberry tree on higher ground and clear of the choking dust. He had a meal ready, and the men came in four at a time to grab a quick bite, change horses, and return to the milling stock.

Starbuck, swapping the gray for a fresh mount, passed up the sorrel and chose instead a strong-looking black; he'd save the sorrel for tomorrow, which likely would be rough, and it would be better to have a horse under him that he knew well.

As he ate his food and waited for Manny to cull the black from the *remuda* he saw Will Vance, Kent, and several others come in. No words passed between them, however. The day had been long and trying, and all were bone-tired and not given to conversation.

Night finally closed, and the land turned from gray and brown to silver and dark shadows as the moon came out to add its light to that shed by the stars. A warm, tense hush settled over the broad swale, broken only by occasional bawls from the herd.

The cattle were not bedding down as they should. Starbuck, walking the black along the fringe of the restless mass, crooning softly as he sought to do his part in soothing them, studied the animals mistrustfully. Most were still on their feet, heads hung low and swinging from side to side. Only a few had elected to graze. It seemed to him that almost the entire herd was poised, ready to break and run at the smallest excuse.

They shouldn't be hurting for water. There had been more than enough for them at the *Brecha* and all had taken their fill. He had been on drives where a herd had gone several days without drinking; it was unusual for this bunch to be in such a jittery state in so short a time.

Shawn turned as two riders, moving slowly and carefully, moved up. They were Gabe and Will Vance. The redhead glanced his way as they passed, and grinned.

"Keep your spurs sharp," he said.

Starbuck smiled and nodded. Farther on he could see the dim outline of another drover, could hear his low, moaning voice. It would be a night like that—one where continual, quiet patrolling would be necessary to keep the cattle reassured and where the riders had to remain alert and ready to move fast if things went wrong. Fortunately, only Kent was new at the job; all of the others were men who knew exactly what must be done.

Tom Zook broke through the slowly settling haze. "Reckon you'd best stay put right here," he said. "Got some of the other boys doing the same. Rest'll be circling. Along about midnight we'll start taking turns sleeping. Critters ought've settled down by then."

Shawn nodded his understanding.

"You want coffee, catch one of the boys and have him set in for you. Don't want Arkansas making the rounds, so you'll have to go after it. A tin cup banging against something could start all hell busting loose."

The foreman rode on, maintaining a slow pace. Shawn settled deeper into his saddle and kneed the black closer to the herd and resumed his crooning. He was dead tired and would be glad when his turn came to rest.

Abruptly, from the corner of his eye, he saw a bright, orange flash behind and to his left. In that same instant a pistol shot split the night's sullen hush. Immediately there was a wild scrambling in the herd beyond him.

Realization came fast—the bushwhacker! He had tried again, and again he had missed, the bullet smashing not into him but hitting instead one of the steers. Shawn had an instantaneous urge to wheel, to send the black racing toward the spot on the slope where he had seen the powder flash.

There was no time. The cattle, startled by the gunshot, were suddenly up and surging forward in a frantic, disorderly mass.

10

Roweling the black, Starbuck rushed toward the wedge of heaving bodies. Somewhere ahead pistols began to sound, and behind him he could hear yelling as the drovers moved to check the flowing sea of cattle and start them milling.

The only hope was to control the lead steers. Abruptly, Shawn pulled away from the flank of the herd and swung toward the yelling at the rear. Almost at once three riders loomed up in the dust-filled gloom.

"Get up front!" he shouted. "Turn the leaders!"

The drovers hesitated, as if reluctant to heed his direction, and then apparently admitting its logic, spurred on by. It would take more than a half a dozen men, however. Low on the black, Starbuck galloped on toward the rear of the herd.

The longhorns were now moving at a dead run, heeding nothing but the animal directly ahead of them, a mighty juggernaut curving from side to side as they followed a path of least resistance. Two riders broke into view.

"Up front!" Shawn yelled. "You can't do a damn thing back here—we've got to turn them!"

In the next moment he recognized Fargo. The man with him was Tom Zook. He grinned his embarrassment as the foreman motioned briskly at him.

"That's where we're headed. Come along, too. I've already got word to the others."

Shawn wheeled, and side by side the three men pounded across the rolling ground for the point. The cattle, no more than fifty yards to their right, raced on, their course an indication that the drovers ahead had so far been unable to change their line of flight. Goaded by thirst and the weather's peculiarities, the longhorns were answering only to an urge to run.

Starbuck twisted half around, unbuckled the straps of his left-hand saddlebag, and pulled out a spare shirt. It was of dark color, and realizing it would not show up to any extent in the pale night, he crammed it back into the leather pouch, and rummaged about until he found a white undershirt. Wedging it under his leg, he secured the buckles and straps again, and then taking the garment by a corner, shook it out full length. He saw Fargo give him a puzzled glance.

"Going to try flagging the lead steers!" he shouted, striving to make himself heard above the thunder of the running herd.

Fargo nodded his understanding and began to peel off his brush jacket. Zook too had caught on and was digging into his saddlebags for something suitable.

They were near the front of the stampede. Other riders began to appear, some with their pistols out and firing ineffectually into the air, others with doubled ropes that they were using as whips. The crazed animals were giving no attention to either.

Starbuck curved off, drew abreast the lead steers, and forged by. A short distance ahead of the pounding, wild-eyed longhorns, he cut the black in on a long tangent. It was dangerous; if his horse stumbled, went down, he'd be finished, but the thought never entered his mind; he could think only of the need to get out in front of the foremost animals, hope to distract and frighten them with the bit of cloth and start them turning.

He reached the center of the point. Two big steers, their wide, pointed horns flashing in the dust particles, were running shoulder to shoulder. Behind them the main body of the herd followed, matching them stride for stride. Shawn spurred the black to where he was just beyond the pair. He wasn't certain what lay on the opposite side of the herd—it could be more flat or it could be a land of broken buttes and treacherous arroyos. But he was fairly sure of level ground to the west, and he could take no chances on losing several hundred head.

More riders began to show up—racing in, shouting, firing their pistols, swinging their ropes. Their faces were barely distinguishable in the choking pall, but he recognized Chesson, Dakan, and the man called Yeager. Shawn raised the undershirt and shook it at them.

"Forget that!" he shouted. "Get something for a flag!"

He didn't wait to see if they complied, but swung in nearer to the dual leaders of the herd, wig-wagging the bit of white cloth frantically.

The pair seemed to slow at his approach, distracted momentarily by the wildly waved undershirt. Beneath him Shawn felt the black tremble as the front rank of cattle swept closer to his hind-quarters. Starbuck spurred him on, edging nearer until he was alongside the right-hand lead steer—a big, wall-eyed brindle with a six-foot spread of needle-sharp horns.

Shifting the shirt to his left hand, holding the reins with the right, he began to slap at the animal's head with the flag. The brute stubbornly held his own for a few yards and then reluctantly started to veer away, crowding against his coleader.

For a time Shawn could hear the clashing of horns above the thudding of hooves as the two steers came together, pitting their strength, and then, almost imperceptibly, the brindle began to have his way and the pair curved slowly off to the left. Behind him Starbuck heard a burst of yelling, and from the tail of an eye, saw the drovers had resorted to flags and were aware of the change.

Holding the black in tight, Starbuck continued to flail away at the brindle, now alone at the head of the herd. The undershirt was little more than a frayed strip as a result of catching upon the steer's horns, but the method was working. The cattle had turned and were now slowing down.

Directly ahead Shawn saw a cluster of riders bearing in on a straight, course. Each had something to use as a flag—jacket, shirt, chaps, a pair of drawers. He had a glimpse of Zook and then of Joe Fargo, his face taut, his snowy hair straggling out from beneath his hat. Pressing close behind were Hubbard and Kent, Crawford and Sim Roberson. The entire crew was now out in front of the herd, he guessed, or else on its right flank, all laboring to force the cattle from their straight-on rush and start them circling.

The black began to falter. Starbuck flung a hasty glance over his shoulder. The steers were running at almost a right angle to the course they had been taking, and already there were some along the flanks that were halting. At once he spurred the lagging horse to the side, pulling away from the herd. The horse had done a good job, and it would be foolhardy to push him, and his own luck, farther.

It was all but over, anyway. Zook, heading up a group of drovers, was hazing the old brindle and the other front runners into a tight spiral as the entire mass, still following stubbornly, gradually slowed.

Starbuck, well off to the side, glanced at the shredded cloth in his hand, smiled ruefully, and tossed it away as he drew the winded black to a halt. He sat motionless for a time, and then dismounting, pulled off his hat and mopped at his dust-caked face. It had been a bad five miles or so, and he hoped they'd been lucky. He'd seen a few steers go down, to be quickly overrun and trampled by the horde behind them, but he didn't think any riders had been lost.

It was said that every herd was destined to stampede at least once on the trail. If such were true perhaps the one ordained for the Diamond J was over and done with and would not occur again. He wished he could feel the same about the bushwhacker's attempts to kill him.

11

The cattle had settled into a closely packed mass. Riders began to appear in the slowly thinning dust as they resumed the chore of patrolling the herd, hopeful of keeping the stock quiet. Starbuck, again astride the now-rested black, doubted there would be any more trouble for the time being, for the longhorns had pretty well run themselves down.

But they were an unpredictable lot, and Shawn, keeping a wary eye on the shadowy slopes, moved at a leisurely trot for the *remuda,* where he would exchange for the gelding. If anything did develop, he wanted a fresh mount under him.

He spotted the spare horses a short distance below the herd, and almost immediately a rider separated from a group nearby and moved forward to intercept him. It was Tom Zook. Starbuck pulled up as the foreman lifted a hand signaling him to halt.

Zook nodded, his features expressionless. "Glad to see you're all right," he said coolly.

Shawn studied the man briefly. Something was bothering him. "Just doing my job."

"Obliged to you for stepping in the way you done. Was no need, however. Had already started shaping up the crew myself."

So that was it—Zook resented his taking over. He shrugged. "Didn't know that at the time."

"Figured that, but I like to keep things straight. I'm bossing the drive. Don't want you to forget it."

"Don't aim to," Starbuck said, his own temper warming. "Anything else?"

"Reckon that covers it."

Shawn rode on, smarting under the foreman's words. Zook had no reason to get riled; he had simply reacted to the moment and gone ahead and done what he thought was necessary. Again his shoulders stirred. It hadn't occurred to him that his actions would appear out of line to Zook. Later, after the matter had cooled down a bit, he'd explain once more. The rope corral of the *remuda* and the cluster of drovers was just ahead. He reined the black toward Manny, who was standing in the opening, and then halted and swung down, aware that all conversation had ceased at his arrival.

"Here's the jaybo you can be thanking for all that hard work."

It was Will Vance. Shawn, in the process of removing his gear preparatory to switching to a fresh horse, paused, anger stirring within him.

"Meaning what?" Zook asked.

Starbuck turned in surprise. He hadn't realized the foreman had followed him back to the *remuda.*

"Meaning that it was him that caused the herd to bust loose and run."

"Afraid you got it wrong—it was a gunshot."

"Sure—fired at him by that bushwhacker that's dogging his tracks."

"That's sort of turning things around, ain't it, Will?" the foreman said, drily. "It wasn't Starbuck that fired the shot."

"Ain't saying it was. Am saying that if he wasn't along there wouldn't be no bushwhacker laying out there in the brush to take a shot at him—and cause all our trouble."

The remaining riders were listening intently, their weariness evident in the slackness of their features, the droop of shoulders.

"Kind of backwards way of figuring things, I'd say. Just about anything would've spooked the herd, touchy as them longhorns were."

"But nothing did. It was that shot," Vance said, not giving an inch. "Was him that caused it, no matter which way you look at it. I'm telling you straight out, Tom, he's a jinx and you ought to do something about it."

Starbuck, leaning against the black's hindquarters, touched the others riders with a glance. "That how you all feel?"

There was a long minute of quiet and then Cal Ligon stirred. "It was that shooting that started them running, but I can't see blaming you."

"Me neither," Yeager added.

The remaining drovers said nothing, simply watching.

Over beyond the horses Arkansas was pulling in with the chuck wagon, driving slowly, carefully, endeavoring to make a minimum of noise.

Shawn swung to Zook. "Up to you. If you think the drive'll go better without me, I'm ready to turn back."

"You'll do no such a goddam thing!" the Diamond J foreman said harshly. "I'm running this outfit—and that jinx talk is nothing but a lot of bull."

Zook hesitated, then glared at the men before him. "What's more, I didn't see none of you in there doing even half the job he done in stopping that stampede. Was him that come up with the idea of flagging the leaders— and it was him that had the guts to ride right in alongside of them to do it."

"We'd a stopped them," Vance mumbled. "Always have before."

"Maybe after another five miles of tallow'd been run off them—and a hundred or more had got themselves tromped to death. As it is we lost no more'n a couple of dozen, and one horse. . . . Now, let me tell you something straight out, Will. You start being half the drover Starbuck is and maybe I'll do some listening to what you've got to say."

The older man bristled. "You want me to quit?"

"Hell, no, I don't want you or nobody else quitting. I'm just telling you to tend to your job and leave the bossing to me."

"Not aiming to—"

"Maybe not, but you're a mite free with your lip and that's something I can do without. Now, all of you, mount up and get out there with the herd. Want them steers kept quiet. We'll be moving at first light, and that ought to put us at the watering place by noon. Once we're there I expect things'll go easier for us."

"Don't bet on it," Vance said, turning toward his horse. "Got a feeling about this drive—a bad feeling—and I ain't never been wrong before. Long as we got this Starbuck around we're going to have trouble. A Jonah always brings bad luck."

"Move on, Will," Zook said quietly, "and keep that kind of talk to yourself." He glanced at the chuck wagon. The cook had a fire going and the smell of coffee was beginning to hang in the clearing air. "If you need a cup of java grab it now—before you start working. Other boys can get theirs after you spell them."

The men began to move off in the direction of the wagon—some going to the saddle, others leading their horses, glad for the few extra minutes on the ground. The long-legged bay Manny had provided for Shawn was ready, and he started to follow. Zook's voice halted him.

"Meant what I said about the job you're doing."

Starbuck studied the foreman coolly. "After what you

77

told me earlier, I—"

"Never mind that. It's just that I believe in keeping everything plain. What I want to say now is that I won't have some old woman like Will Vance with his crazy notions driving you off. Ain't often I can hire on a man with your cow savvy. Asking you to give me your word you'll stick."

Shawn hesitated. "Some truth in what he told you. That bushwhacker'll try again. Could happen at the wrong time."

"Could be the wrong time for him, too. With more'n a dozen of us moving around, somebody's bound to spot him. You think of that?"

"No—"

"Well, think about it. Just could be we'll turn up that jasper before he gets to try again. You can be damn sure the boys'll keep their eyes open—just for their own sake. You get any kind of a squint at him when he fired that shot?"

"Saw the powder flash. Came from back of me and up on a slope. I started after him but the cattle broke loose right then and I had other things to do."

"Obliged to you for looking at it that way."

"Figure the job you're paying me to do comes first."

Tom Zook nodded, smiling. "Reckon Joe was right about you. Now, go on, get yourself some java. Anybody starts bad-mouthing you, tell them to go do their yammering at me. It's a part of the bossing chore—listening to sore-assed cowpunchers bitch. That clear?"

"Clear," Starbuck said, and swinging onto the bay, headed for the chuck wagon.

12

The herd, with the old brindle steer again at its head, was up and moving long before the yellow flare of sunrise had replaced the sullen gray of first light.

Starbuck, wearied by the stampede and the subsequent hours of close vigil, fell into position beside the moving cattle. Once the longhorns were underway, riders began to doze on their saddles, exhaustion finally catching up with them.

But there was no such relief for Shawn. The presence of the bushwhacker made rest an impossibility for him. At any moment the crack of a pistol might be heard again, and a bullet come racing out of the nearby brush or from behind a mound of rocks to cut him down.

There was no place to hide even if he had the inclination. He was out in the open, with no choice other than to do his job of riding alongside the lumbering longhorns, and despite the hovering dust, he knew he was an easy target.

He took no comfort in Zook's statement that the killer would now find it more difficult to pursue his intentions because of the vigilance aroused in the other drovers. The men were worn out and could be expected to do no more than look after their own interests; besides, being on the watch would prove of no value in halting a bullet, once fired.

And Shawn wasn't so sure it mattered to the riders. Will Vance had made it clear how he, and undoubtedly many more, felt about his presence on the drive. They were fully convinced that only trouble and bad luck could be the result. Certainly, they would take little interest in his well-being.

"Just can't figure what's got into Will," Joe Fargo said around mid-morning when they were riding together. "Like I told you, he always was sort of spooky about some things, but this, well, it plain don't make no sense."

"Got to admit that it was that bushwhacker taking a shot at me that started the stampede."

"Sure, but if Will's looking to blame somebody, he ought to blame him, not you. Was him that pulled the trigger."

"Way he sees it, and I expect there's a few others feeling the same way, if I wasn't around, there wouldn't be somebody out there using a gun."

"Still ain't right—and Zook ain't seeing it like that. Right now you're the fair-headed boy in his tally book."

There was a note of pride in the old drover's voice, occasioned, Shawn supposed, by the fact that he had been vouched for by Fargo.

"If you'd heard him making it plain to me that he was trail-bossing this herd, you would've gotten a different idea," he said wryly.

Fargo's thick brows lifted in surprise, and then he laughed. "Sounds like Tom, all right. Always was one to let folks know what's what. But don't misfigure him. He seen you jump in right quick and do what had to be done without no dilly-dallying, and he liked it. Heard from Cal Ligon that he took Will down a couple a notches this morning."

"There were a few words passed. Didn't help the way

Vance feels about me."

"Nothing would, I expect," Fargo said, yawning widely. "And it'll be like that all the way to Dodge."

"Which sure isn't good. Crew hadn't ought to be split, specially this early in the drive. . . . How long before we come to that water? Cattle are getting jumpy again."

"Couple more hours. When we reach it, Tom wants to hold over a spell, then push on. We hit the main trail north tomorrow, and the next day we'll come to the Brazos. Things ought to go all right once we cross it."

If that bushwhacker will stay clear of me, Shawn thought.

As if reading his mind Fargo said, "You seen any signs of that jasper? The one trying to plug you, I mean."

Starbuck shook his head. "Biding his time," he said, and then spurring on, added, "see you later."

The clouds to the southeast seemed to be thickening, he noted as he worked his way alongside the herd. A good, cooling shower would be most welcome—and if it came, he hoped it would be just that and not one of those crackling, thunder-pounding storms that could make matters worse instead of better.

He could feel the tension among the men as he circled the cattle, and missed none of the dark, side looks that came his way. The seeds of dissension sown by Will Vance had found fertile ground among the drovers, at least among most of them, and it brought a stir of dissatisfaction to Shawn.

It was wrong to jeopardize the welfare of the herd, and he decided suddenly that he'd not let it continue. True, he'd given his word to Tom Zook that he would stay, but that could be changed; at the first town they came to where help could be hired he'd tell the trail boss he was quitting. Zook might not like it but he'd have to admit that it was the only thing to be done.

It was near noon when they reached Indian Creek. The longhorns smelled the water miles before it was in sight, and broke into a lope. When they came to the all-too-small stream, they fairly overran it, converting it quickly into a muddy swamp, but there was enough water available to satisfy their needs. Zook called a stopover, a welcome break during which the drovers had time to eat a good meal and grab some rest, and then around the middle of the afternoon he gave the order to move on.

The steers were reluctant and held back stubbornly, continually cutting off in singles and doubles and small jags seeking to return to the water hole. But the riders kept after them, and finally they were all in motion, flowing across a wide, grassy flat beneath the hot sky.

Starbuck, laboring with the rest, found himself at one time riding with Kent on one side and Will Vance on the other. Neither had any words for him and he guessed the younger man had joined the ranks of those viewing him in the same light as Vance. He passed it off with a shrug; it would all come to an end at the next town, and Vance and his followers could stop worrying about having a jinx in the party.

As he rode, Shawn found himself looking over his shoulder, scouring the adjacent country for evidence of a rider keeping pace with the herd—and hoping to find an opportunity for getting another shot at him. There was ample cover—clumps of stunted trees, long strips of thick brush, an occasional upthrust of rocks—but he saw no one.

It was difficult to understand why the killer didn't take advantage of it and the only explanation he could come up with was that the man preferred darkness, when escape would be easier. That he was still around, some- where, and would make his move again when the proper moment presented itself, was a foregone conclusion.

Such thoughts set Starbuck to wondering once more who the man could be and what had set him on his quest for vengeance. The question had never fully been out of his mind from the moment of the first attempt, but he found he could still not answer it.

And it was dangerous to let it ride, as he was doing now. He should take steps to force the killer's hand, make him come out into the open. He shouldn't continue to simply drift along, hoping to escape a bullet in the back. That was another good and valid reason for quitting the drive; once he relieved himself of his obligations to Tom Zook, he'd be free to act on his own behalf.

They halted that night in a broad valley deep in grass, and the tired cattle, their thirsts slaked, quartered well. Zook broke the crew into three four-hour watches. This gave each man ample time for sleep.

When the drive began again the next day, under a sky gradually filling with clouds, everyone was in much better condition—physically and mentally.

"First couple of days are always the worst," Joe Fargo said as, late in the afternoon, they came in sight of the Brazos River, "but I reckon you know that. Cattle's just got to get it into their heads what it's all about, and drovers always sort've got to get acquainted. That's one reason Tom likes to hire on as many of the same bunch as he can every year. . . . Will still got that burr in his drawers?"

Shawn nodded. "Along with most every other man in the crew. I'm quitting first town we come to."

"Quitting?" Concern spread over the old puncher's rugged features. "Hell, you can't do that!"

"Can and will."

"You told Tom yet?"

"No."

Fargo pulled off his hat and brushed at the shock of white hair capping his head. "I sure am sorry to hear you say that, boy. Had some things in mind I aimed to talk over with you. Didn't you give Tom your word you'd stay?"

"I'm asking it back. I can't let things go along like they are. Crew'll be at each other's throats in another day or two—and we're a long way from Dodge. Besides, I aim to find out who it is that's gunning for me and settle with him. I'm not about to keep going on, looking back over my shoulder every few minutes to see if I'm being trailed."

"Can savvy that," Fargo said. "Maybe we can talk Tom into letting us both off for a couple of days so's we can do some scouting around, once we've got the herd across the river."

"He can't spare anybody. This bunch of steers is too jumpy, and he needs all the help he's got. I'll wait until he gets somebody in my place. No need for you to stick your neck out, anyway."

"Maybe I got personal reasons," the older man said, cocking his head to one side.

"Appreciate that," Starbuck replied, "but I'd best go it alone." He passed off Joe's statement as merely an expression of interest based on the fact that Fargo had been the one to recommend him to Zook in the first place, and now felt some responsibility.

Joe Fargo sighed. "Well, sure do hate to see you pull out, but I reckon we'd better quit yammering and get up front, help push these critters across to the other side of the river. Can do some more talking later."

The stream was low and the herd moved into it willingly enough, holding back only to drink as the water slapped around their flanks. The old brindle steer, seemingly aware of his self-assumed leadership, led them on a straight line to the opposite shore, and in a surprisingly short time the entire herd of cattle was on solid ground.

"Sure never figured it'd be that easy," Charlie Hubbard said as he rode drag with Starbuck, Fargo, and two others sometime later. "Usually fighting the danged things ever step of the way."

"River's higher'n this, mostly. Always been plenty of raining going on—not like this year," Fargo said. He paused, raised himself in his stirrups, and craned his neck at a rider coming back along the flank of the herd at a hard gallop.

Pulling to the side, he yelled, "What's the trouble, Norm? You're moving like the devil flies was after you!"

"Got to get Arkansas," the man shouted as he swept by. "Tom's horse's throwed him. Thinks he's busted his shoulder."

13

Fargo swore deeply. Charlie Hubbard stroked his whiskery chin. "Maybe Will's right. Maybe this here is a hard-luck drive." The drover caught himself, looked quickly at Shawn. "Not meaning that at you, of course."

"Now, that there's a barrel of horse feathers if ever I heard of any!" Fargo snapped. "It ain't got nothing to do with him and you know it! Come on, best we go see Tom."

The two men spurred away. Shawn paused to look back toward the chuck wagon, still on the other side of the river. The puncher that had gone for Arkansas had given over his horse to the cook, who was now pounding for the crossing, his faded green carpetbag of medical supplies clutched tightly in one hand.

Starbuck waited until the elderly man had passed, and then dropping back to see that the herd was moving as it should, he made the quick survey of the nearby country that had become habitual with him. Seeing no one suspicious, he rode on toward the front of the herd. He found Tom Zook, with Arkansas working over his left arm and shoulder, while Fargo and the majority of the crew looked on.

Standing in the center of the group was Will Vance, his seamy features set and angry. He glanced up as Shawn halted and dismounted, but he made no comment.

"Busted, all right," the cook said. "How'd it happen?"

A long, gusty breath slipped from the foreman's lips. "Goddammed horse stepped in a hole."

"Ain't nothing to do but get yourself to a doc somewheres," Arkansas said, pointing to some bits of drift-wood a short distance to the side. "One of you fetch me a piece of that—something I can use to splint him up with."

Hubbard hurriedly procured the desired length of wood, and the cook set to work. Zook—his features contorted with pain and teeth clenched—stared straight ahead. He made no sound while Arkansas bound him so that there could be no movement of the broken bone. When it was finished, he reached up with his free hand and brushed away the sweat beading his forehead. Only then did he speak.

"By God, I'm sure glad you're done! You make a damn sight better cook than you do a sawbones—that's for certain."

Arkansas shrugged, returning the leftover strips of cloth he'd used as bandages to his bag. "Ain't never laid no claim to being a doctor," he said mildly. "Was hired on to cook. . . . Now, you ain't to move that there arm, no matter what."

"Move it! For crissake, you got me so trussed up I can hardly breathe, much less move!"

"Way it's supposed to be, and the quicker you get to a doc and get that bone set right, better it'll be. Hear?"

Tom Zook's angry impatience began to fade. "Yeh, I hear. Means Abilene. It's the closest."

Arkansas nodded. "Then best you head on back to the ranch. That doc ain't going to want you doing no riding."

Aided by one of the drovers, the foreman struggled to his feet. Anger again sparked his eyes. "Of all the goddam lousy luck—"

"What I told you to be looking for," Vance said quietly. "We got us a hoodoo, and this kind of a thing ain't going to quit until we get rid—"

"Shut up, Will," Fargo cut in harshly. "You know there ain't no truth in what you're saying."

"I know things just keep popping up—like this—and there ain't no reason for it."

"Well, it's plain foolish to go blaming Starbuck or anybody else. Happened, that's all."

"Which is how it is," Zook said, "the sooner some of you get them crazy notions about hoodoos and jinxes out of your head, the better it will be because you're going to be taking orders from the man."

Starbuck drew up slowly, eyes narrowing as he considered the foreman. Directly across, Will Vance pushed a full step forward, face darkening.

"What's that?"

"You heard me. Since I won't be making the rest of the drive, I'm naming a trail boss to take my place."

"Starbuck?" Vance asked in a taut voice.

"Him," Zook replied, bobbing his head.

"Not me," Shawn said quickly. "Pick somebody else."

"Ain't nobody else that can handle it."

"Bound to be. Plenty in this crew that are older than me and that've had more experience."

"No doubt. Didn't you say that you'd done a turn or two bossing a drive?"

"Yes, but this is different. You've got some drovers working for you that have made this drive before. Give them the chance."

"That ain't all there is to heading up a drive—being

older and knowing the way—and if they're honest they'll be the first to tell you I'm right. Trail-bossing is a round-the-clock job, and it takes a man who can think fast, and act faster. I've seen you work and it makes you my choice. I'm right, ain't I, boys?"

"Yes, sir," Fargo said promptly.

A half a dozen others joined in with the old rider in their approval. Will Vance and those standing by him made no answer. Zook fixed the squat drover with a pressing glare.

"I'm waiting to hear from you, mister."

Vance shrugged. "No sense asking me that. You know how I feel."

"I know you got a tick in your hide that's making you sore as a galled mule, but that ain't the question. I'm saying there ain't a better man to take over than Starbuck. You ready to say there is?"

"I don't want the job," Shawn cut in stubbornly before Vance could reply. "Fact is, I aimed to quit first town we come to if you were willing to give me back my word."

"Which I ain't—and won't," Zook said, shifting painfully. "Got to hold you to it. The buyer's waiting in Dodge for the herd, and I figure you're the one that can get it there. Hell, you won't have no trouble. Some of the drovers you got are the best in the country."

"Sure," Fargo said heartily, "ain't no reason to worry none. We'll all stand by you."

Starbuck, unmoved, shook his head stubbornly. "You'd better pick somebody else. I'll stay on, if that'll help, do my share."

"Want you calling the turn, not riding herd." Zook was

no less insistent. "And that's how it's to be, so cut out the palavering." He shifted his eyes to Vance and the men standing by him.

"I'm counting on every one of you to keep right on doing your work same as if it was me running things. Any man not sticking to the bargain he made when he signed on will answer to me later. Nobody's to quit and nobody's to question Starbuck's orders. Anybody does any of them things, he's not only through ever working for Diamond J but I'll spread word to ever rancher I know that he ain't to be hired on because he ain't dependable. I make myself clear?"

Vance continued his silence. Gabe, his broad face sober, shook his head. "Reckon it'll be however you say, Mister Zook. I ain't hankering to lose that job you promised me when we get back. Howsomever, it does seem—"

"Seem what?" the foreman demanded when the rider paused uncertainly.

"Well, that there's a powerful lot of bad luck going on."

"And you think Starbuck's the cause of it?"

"Was him that got the stampede going—leastwise, it was that shot somebody took at him. And now, your horse falling—"

"You're talking like you was a five-year-old kid, or maybe a hundred-and-five-year-old squaw. Makes no sense at all. Starbuck's got himself a personal problem, but I reckon he can take care of it. You just see to doing your part in getting this herd up the trail to Dodge. That's all you need study on."

"Yes, sir—"

Zook glanced around questioningly. No one spoke. "All right, I take it everything's settled. We'll night here and you can get an early start in the morning. Amos, you and Dakan drop back across the river, help Arkansas bring the shuttler. Rest of you see to bedding down the herd—and pass the word along to them that wasn't here about Starbuck taking over. Any of them want to jaw about it, tell them I'll be waiting right here."

The riders started to turn away, Shawn with them. He halted at Zook's voice.

"Not you, Starbuck. We've got some business to tend to. Want to turn the selling papers over to you and give you the word on how things are to be handled when you get to Dodge." The foreman paused and touched his bound arm gently. "Goddam thing's sure giving me fits. . . . You ready to listen?"

Shawn shrugged, reluctant to the last. "Ready as I'll ever be," he said, heavily.

14

"I sure ain't liking the looks of that," Joe Fargo said that next morning as he stared at the eastern horizon. Beyond the rolling rim in the distance the first rays of the sun were flooding the sky with deep red.

Shawn paused, threw his gaze to the south. The clouds had thickened, and were now an ever-growing gray mass. The long overdue rains were about to arrive. Turning to his saddle, he freed the slicker from the strings that secured it behind the cantle. Elsewhere along the rope corral other men, glum and voiceless in the cool dimness, were making similar preparations.

It was more than the early hour that laid a sullen restraint upon them, Shawn knew. They resented him and the fact that he had been chosen to take over the drive—some because of his youth, others, those who sided Will Vance, because they believed his presence could only mean more trouble.

He was doing his best to ignore it. He had not wanted the job in the first place and had accepted it simply because he'd had no other choice. But now that the responsibility was his he would do his best to get the cattle to Dodge City without undue losses, and in the process he was determined to brook no interference. He had stated that position to Zook before he had ridden out for Abilene, and the Diamond J foreman had said he would back him all the way.

There were a few of the drovers he felt certain he could rely upon—Fargo, Hubbard, Yeager, Amos Green, and probably Kent, who was still pretty much under Charlie Hubbard's wing. Arkansas and Manny, the wrangler, too, appeared willing to cooperate. There were others who were not making their feelings known, but as time wore on their status would become clear.

The sorrel ready, Starbuck paused and glanced toward the chuck wagon. The last of the riders were finishing their breakfasts. After they were gone, Arkansas would remain where he was and await the men who had been on the final leg of the night shift, now in the process of being relieved. Once they were fed he would then load up the shuttler and follow the herd.

"Soon as we get the cattle moving, I'll be riding on

ahead," he said to Fargo as he swung to the saddle. "Noticed yesterday the country's pretty well grazed over. Been quite a few herds pass this way. Want to see if the grass is any better farther west."

The older man studied him thoughtfully. "You aiming to go alone?"

Shawn nodded. "Want every man we've got working the herd. Cattle never have settled down good."

Fargo scrubbed at his jaw. "That's sure a fact. About the orneriest bunch of critters I've seen in a long time. . . . Ain't so sure you taking off by yourself is such a good idea. That bushwhacker—"

"Forget him," Starbuck snapped impatiently. "Got no time to worry about him."

"You just better take time, maybe."

Shawn's manner softened. "I'll be on the lookout. Going to depend on you seeing that things go all right while I'm gone."

"Sure. How long'll that be?"

"Three, four hours. No more than that."

Starbuck looked around as the first of the night herders rode in to the wagon. They passed by, faces tipped down—Dakan, Cass Walton, and Sim Roberson. None of them gave any sign of recognition. Shawn's features hardened but he said nothing. Bringing his attention back to Joe Fargo, he bobbed his head.

"Let's move them out," he said, and swung off in the direction of the herd.

Near mid-morning Starbuck halted on a low rise some five miles or so west of the main trail. As he had hoped, there had been less traffic across that particular part of the country, and grazing conditions were much better. It would be wise to pull the cattle off the customary route followed and use the one paralleling it. He'd start the changeover as soon—

Shawn's thoughts came to a halt. A distance to his right, in a brush-lined arroyo, motion had caught his eye. At once he touched the gelding with his spurs, sending him down the slope. His hand dropped quickly to the pistol on his hip.

The bushwhacker?

He considered the question coolly as he rode without haste in a direct line for the point that had attracted him. If it were, this was the moment to have it out, to settle whatever it was on the would-be killer's mind. Spending another two weeks or better on the trail, and being ever on the watch, was something he had no taste for. Better to finish it now.

The sorrel's stride broke. His ears came forward to sharp points, relaxing as he continued at a slower pace. Starbuck's hand wrapped around the butt of the forty-five, forefinger slipping into the trigger guard to rest upon the curved bit of steel as his thumb hooked over the weapon's hammer. He felt the wet warmness of sweat under his collar as a prickling ran along his spine. At that instant the bushwhacker could be sighting down a gun barrel, centering him as he approached.

It would be an easy shot. He was a fool to yield to impulse, to the deep anger that had sprung into being that first day when the bushwhacker had made the initial attempt on his life and that had never fully dissipated. He should have played it smart, acted as if he had not noticed the man's presence, ridden off quickly into the opposite direction and then circled back. Now, he was moving straight at the killer, hoping to get off the first shot—but in his present frame of mind Shawn Starbuck had taken none of that into consideration; he had, as was his way, challenged the problem head on.

The tangled wall of brush was immediately before him. Starbuck halted the sorrel, a frown pulling at his set features. The killer should have made his move by that moment. Tense, pistol now cocked and ready, he kneed the gelding to the left, to a break in the undergrowth, and rode him down into the arroyo.

There was no one there. He swore softly. That his nerves were honed to a razor's edge was undeniable, but he knew he hadn't reached the point where he was imagining things. Besides, the sorrel had either heard or seen something.

He glanced up and down the wash. It extended both north and south for twenty or thirty yards, and then was lost to his view as it curved away. Could the bushwhacker have changed his mind for some reason?

Dropping from the saddle, Starbuck moved forward to the point where he had seen motion. A grunt of satisfaction broke from his tight lips. There, in the dry, sun-baked sand were hoof prints where a horse had stood. He hadn't been wrong; a rider had watched him from behind the screen of brush—watched, and then for some reason, had pulled out.

Raising his glance, he studied the floor of the wash. The sand was loose, and though impressions left upon it disappeared almost as quickly as made, he found what he sought—the faint marks here and there of a horse moving off down the arroyo.

Pivoting, he vaulted onto the saddle, and roweling the gelding hastily, sent him racing along the narrow channel at the top speed. Whoever it was could not be too far ahead. Only a few minutes, at most, could have elapsed since he had first spotted what was to have been an ambush.

A quarter hour later, with the sorrel heaving from the labor of running through the loose sand, Shawn reined in. The arroyo had worked itself onto level ground and become lost in an area of low, knobby hills. There was no sign of a rider.

Disappointment stirred through Starbuck, and then again spurring the gelding, he crossed a narrow swale and climbed to a higher ridge for a look at the country farther on. It was inconceivable a man could cover that much ground in so short a time, but he would have his look, nevertheless.

There was no one to be seen. As near as he could tell he was the only person within miles—but that possibly was an illusion; there were countless patches of brush and innumerable small hills, all of which offered concealment for a man wishing to hide. The bushwhacker, if that was who it had been, could be anywhere, and he could search until nightfall without finding him.

The puzzling thing was why the killer, the advantage all his, had chosen to pass up the opportunity. Shawn could think of only one answer; the man had no stomach for a face-to-face encounter, preferring instead to make his kill from behind or under cover of night.

Twisting about, Starbuck looked to the east, getting his bearings, and then wheeling the sorrel, he began a long tangent that would enable him to intercept the herd.

A moment later his head came up sharply. From somewhere in the distance two quick gunshots sounded, the echoes floating hollowly through the warm air of the overcast day. He hung motionless for a long moment pondering their meaning, and then abruptly put the gelding once more into a fast lope. The shots had come from the direction of the herd; it could only mean trouble.

15

Joe Fargo rode to the edge of the dust stirred up by the herd and pulled to a halt, his squinting eyes on Starbuck's receding figure. He was wishing Shawn had permitted him to go along on the search for better grass, but the big, quiet-faced rider had refused to listen, insisting that he stay with the cattle and keep them moving.

Fargo remained motionless, slumped forward, an elbow resting on his saddle horn until Starbuck was lost in the short hills to the west, and then he turned back to the cattle plodding along sluggishly in the early morning coolness.

He was sorry now that he had said anything to Tom Zook about Shawn being a good prospect for a trail boss job—a natural, had been the way he put it. It had come up not long ago after the stampede, during casual conversation and had been meant merely as an offhand remark. He had no idea then, of course, that Tom would get hurt, and even less that the Diamond J foreman would tap Starbuck to fill his boots when the need arose. His comments likely were of no great consequence, anyway; Zook had recognized Shawn's ability without having it pointed out to him.

But it wasn't good. Starbuck, saddled with a mighty big problem of his own, hadn't wanted the job, and certainly hadn't sought it as some of the crew seemed to think. He'd even tried to quit rather than create any problems on the drive, only Tom wouldn't hear of it—even went so far as to exact a promise from him to stay on. And of course Shawn, being the kind of man he was, honored his word.

Starbuck was a square-shooter, all right, Fargo told himself, and he sure hoped he could work something out with him along the lines he'd mentioned to Jenny; but he'd not be going into it just yet. Shawn had too much on his mind. They had a long way to go yet before they reached Dodge, and Will Vance and his bunch were setting out to make it tough by laying down on the job.

Up ahead on the left flank of the herd a dozen or more steers had split off and halted to graze. Two of the drovers, Ligon and Cass Walton, were nearby but were paying no mind, simply passing them by. Suddenly angry, Fargo spurred up to them.

"What the hell's the matter with you jaspers?" he demanded. "Don't you see them critters a-wandering off?"

Ligon took the dead cigarette hanging from a corner of his mouth and flipped it aside. "Expect they'll catch up when they take the notion," he said, shrugging indifferently.

"Maybe they will and maybe they won't!" Fargo snapped. "You're getting paid to keep them bunched—and I want to see you doing it."

Walton grinned. "Yes, sir, Mister Fargo."

"Then get back there and chase them into line. Herd's moving too slow, anyhow."

Abruptly the older man cut away, and still glowering, loped toward the rear. He caught sight of the punchers riding drag. Bandana masks pushed down under their chins, they had pulled off to one side to avoid the hanging dust.

"What're you doing out here?" he shouted. "Get yourselves back there where you belong—and start pushing that herd. We're moving too slow."

He didn't wait to hear a response but continued on for the opposite flank. Irritation again rocked him. Several steers had wandered from the main body of the drive and were scattered about nipping aimlessly at the thin grass, raising their heads now and then to look at a stand of trees farther east.

Five men, still in their saddles, were halted a distance above them, engaged in a discussion of some sort. Roweling his horse, Fargo hurried toward them. As he drew near he swore in disgust; he might've guessed—one was Will Vance. The others were Sim Roberson and Troy Dakan, who seemed to be involved in an argument, and Yeager and Norm Crawford, who, like Vance, were looking on.

"What the hell is this?" Fargo asked, drawing to a halt.

Vance smiled thinly. "Troy and Sim's just settling a little problem, that's all. Seems there was some gal back in San Angelo—"

"Forget it!" Fargo cut in. "You all are supposed to be working. Now, get at it—all of you!"

Will Vance lifted his thick brows and smiled again. "You heard the straw boss," he drawled. "We best get back to droving."

"I ain't doing nothing till Troy's willing to say he's a liar," Roberson muttered.

The dark-faced Dakan shook his head slowly. "You'll see me frying in hell before I do."

Immediately Fargo stepped in between the two. This was more than just an ordinary difference of opinion. All the signs of real trouble were there.

"This here's stopping right now," he said. "Troy, I'm needing you over on the other flank. Get yourself there fast, help Ligon and Walton. . . . Sim, I can use you at point. Move out—both of you!"

Dakan spun, cutting back through the dust for the west side of the herd. Roberson, features sullen, watched until the rider was gone from sight, and then spurring his horse, he loped toward the front of the drive.

"Rest of you," the old puncher said, facing the others, "get after them strays and stay after them. Don't want to see no more hanging back. Hear?"

Vance nodded. "Sure. . . . Say, where's the hoodoo?"

"Be enough of that!" Fargo snarled, anger growing with each passing moment.

"You mean me calling him a hoodoo? Hell, there ain't no need for me to say it. Proving itself—the stampede, Tom getting all busted up, everybody fussing the way they are."

"You ain't helping none, blabbering about it all the time!"

"Just saying what's true and what everybody can see for hisself."

"They wouldn't be seeing it if you'd quit putting it in their heads. Now, start rounding up them strays before we lose them."

"Sure, Joe, but you're dodging my question. Where's the big trail boss?"

"Looking for better grass."

"That so? Nobody went with him?"

"Nope. Rode off alone."

"Well, what d'you know!" Vance said, grinning widely. "Maybe we'll get lucky—maybe that bushwhacker'll show up again and do some straight shooting this time. Then we'll be shed of that—"

"I won't let you go talking about him like that, Will," Fargo broke in, his voice low and even. "Want you to hush up. And far as the job's concerned, you know the same as me he didn't want it. Tried to quit, in fact, only Tom wouldn't let him. So's he's going ahead, making the best of it and doing what he ought. Was you the right kind of a man, you'd be helping him, not crucifying him the way you are."

"Can't fault me if he's a Jonah," the drover said, and abruptly pulled off.

Yeager and Crawford remained motionless for a few moments and then, wheeling, followed. Fargo brushed at the sweat on his face, sighing heavily. Matters were rapidly getting out of hand, and it would take very little to blow the whole works sky high as far as the crew was concerned. And it was all a bunch of dang foolishness—a mess of nothing. But drovers were strange critters; they were all the time getting some loco notion in their heads, and it usually took the devil himself to get it out.

Coming around, Fargo mopped his face again and swung back across the drag, having his look at Arkansas and the chuck wagon. The cook was slowly making his way, still far enough away to be outside the dust pall. Everything appeared to be all right with him. Farther back Manny and the *remuda* were advancing as expected.

Pointing for the front of the herd, Fargo rode its length, noting as he did that the strays had been hazed into line and that the cattle were moving a bit faster. Near the point he caught up with Charlie Hubbard and paused to have a few words with him. Charlie was one that could be depended upon to do his part, and he guessed that Kent, his young friend, would do likewise. If things would just go right for a couple of days, maybe all the trouble would blow over.

He rode on, drawing abreast the front rank of steers. The brindle was a few lengths ahead of the others. He'd established himself as the herd's leader and was not relinquishing the post to any of his kind—and he was doing a good job of it. Roy Chesson wheeled from point center and dropped back to his side.

"What's eating on Sim Roberson? Showed up here a while back burning like pitch pine."

Joe shrugged wearily. "Him and Dakan's got something slanchways in their craw. Had to pull them apart. Sent Troy over to work the left flank. Figured you could keep Sim busy up here. Where's he now?"

Chesson pushed his hat to the back of his head and glanced about. "Danged if I know. Was here a bit ago."

Two quick gunshots suddenly rolled across the rumble of the moving herd. Fargo stiffened and flung a worried glance at the cattle. They seemed not to have noticed. He turned back to Chesson.

"What do you reckon that meant?"

"Come from over there," the puncher said, pointing to the left. A frown drew his brows together. "You don't think maybe that Sim and Troy—"

Fargo didn't answer. Driving spurs into his horse, he cut away from the herd, which was now finally reacting to the reports and breaking into a slow run. Two of the drovers wheeled to follow him, evidently also having heard the shots. He waved them back into place.

"Keep them steers going straight!" he yelled, and rushed on, eyes now fixed on a cluster of riders that had halted off to the side.

"It's them—"

He hadn't noticed that Hubbard was following. Nodding, he pulled to a halt. Sim Roberson lay on the ground near his horse, a broad stain on his shirt front. Dakan, a half a dozen strides away, was thumbing a fresh cartridge into his pistol. Ligon, Walton, and Amos Green, still mounted, were looking on in a surprised sort of way.

Fargo came off the saddle hurriedly, knelt beside the prostrate man, and made a brief examination. Rising, he glanced at Dakan.

"Sim's dead."

Troy Dakan shrugged, sliding his weapon back into the

holster. "Drawed on me. I got there first."

"That's what it was," Ligon said. "A fair fight."

Joe Fargo swore deeply. Trouble was a long way from being over, it seemed. Half turning, he motioned to Hubbard.

"Ride over to the wagon and get us a couple of shovels. We'll bury Sim there by them bushes. Rest of you, get back to the cattle—"

"Not me," Dakan said flatly. "I'm leaving."

"Why? Boys say it was a fair fight."

"Ain't that. I plumb had enough of this here drive. It's a Jonah for certain."

"Hell, you can't blame this on the drive," Fargo said, his voice heavy with disgust. "Was your own doings, nobody else's."

"Not how I figure it. Sim was my best friend," Dakan replied, and mounted his horse, headed south over the route they had been traveling.

1 6

Starbuck saw the herd first. It was moving along at a fair pace, but not a hard run. Relief flowed through him. The shots, whatever they were, had not caused another stampede. His attention shifted to a small cluster of men near the chuck wagon, which had been halted near a low bluff. At once he veered toward them, a tautness gripping him as he drew near and saw the blanket-covered figure on the ground. Reining in, he dismounted and faced Joe Fargo.

"Who is it?"

"Sim Roberson," the old puncher replied.

"What happened?"

"Him and Dakan got in a argument. He come out second best. . . . Dakan's gone."

Shawn glanced at the men gathered to bury the drover. Only about a third of the crew were present. Two of them were hollowing out a trench in the hard ground for a grave. Either the remaining riders had already been there to pay their respects, or Fargo had insisted they not leave the herd.

"That'll do, boys."

Fargo's laconic comment brought a stop to the digging. Chesson and Hubbard laid aside their shovels and took places at each end of the shrouded corpse. Lifting carefully, they lowered it into the depression and stepped back, removing their broad-brimmed hats as they did. The others followed suit, and Fargo, turning, looked expectantly at Arkansas. The cook, his whiskery face pink in the driving sunlight, crossed to the head of the grave and turned his eyes upward.

"Lord, reckon there ain't much I can say about Sim Roberson, him being a close-mouthed man and never talking much about himself, but he was straight and he was friendly and he was good to his horse.

"Don't know what was bothering him and caused this ruckus that got him killed, but I expect he figured he was right, so I guess he had a call coming. Now, if You're willing, we'll all be mighty grateful if You'll let him through the Pearly Gates without no fussing. Amen."

Arkansas moved back, Hubbard and Chesson replaced their hats, and taking up their shovels, began to fill in the trench. Starbuck, jaw set, drew off to one side and beckoned to Fargo.

"Must be a bit more to this than what you told me."

The older man shrugged. "You heard it all. They got to bickering. Don't know what was said, but it must've been a mite strong. I pulled them apart once and sent them off so there'd be plenty of ground between them. Next thing I knowed, there was shooting and old Sim was dead."

"Never noticed any trouble between them before?"

"There wasn't—fact is, they was good friends. Trouble just sort've jumped up between them."

The inference in Fargo's words and tone, intentional or otherwise, was not lost on Starbuck. His eyes narrowed.

"I'm being blamed for it, I take it. Wasn't for me they wouldn't have got to quarreling—same as there wouldn't have been a stampede or Zook wouldn't have broken his shoulder."

"Well, since you're asking straight out, I reckon there's some blaming you—"

"Most—"

Fargo stirred uncomfortably. "Yeh, guess a man could say most. Was the reason Dakan pulled out, too. Had no cause to do it except he's been listening to Vance."

"That this is a hard-luck drive—and I'm a hoodoo."

"That's it. And if things like this keep happening, it'll get worse."

Shawn swore helplessly. "I know that, and if there was anything I could do about, I sure as hell would . . . but how do you go about it?"

"You don't," Fargo said. "None of it's your fault in the

first place. Things just up and happen on a drive. You find what you was hunting for?"

Shawn nodded, his attention moving to the riders, who with the exception of Hubbard and Chesson, were mounted now and starting back to the herd. Their eyes, sullen and filled with resentment, touched him. Beyond them Arkansas was using the back of a shovel to drive a crude cross into the hard ground at the head of the grave.

"Plenty of grass about five miles west. Aim to begin turning the cattle that direction today."

"What kind of country is it?"

"Pretty much flat, like this. Some hills, but we won't have any problems."

"Be smart was we to stay clear of the hills," Fargo said, and then cocked his head to one side. "You spot anybody else around?"

Starbuck could see no need to mention the bush-whacker, or what he thought was him; he could have been wrong. And if word got out that the killer was close, it would create more tension.

"Been nobody through there in quite a spell," he said, making it only a half lie. "Any trouble while I was gone?"

"Some of the crew dogging it. Got on them right smart."

"Been expecting that, and I aim to have a talk with the whole crew when we stop. Not going to lose any sleep over me, but I'm not about to let them fall down on Tom—or Justice. There a town anywhere close where I might hire on some drovers?"

"Other side of the Pease River. Place about ten mile

east of the crossing—be a little more'n that if we're moving west."

"What's it called?"

"Powder Keg."

"Any chance I can do some hiring there?"

"Maybe. Ain't much of a place—saloon, couple of houses, a store. Just might find somebody laying around willing to work, howsomever."

"I'll ride over tomorrow, if need be," Starbuck said, and turned back to the sorrel. "Pass the word on that we're swinging west. I'll go up front, get them started."

Mounting, he angled across the flat toward the herd, now again moving at the usual pace. Pulling in alongside, he came abreast two of the drovers and spoke. Their response was a cool nod. Temper simmering, he rode on, face stiff, shoulders square against the sun. A third rider appeared in the dusty haze . . . Kent. Starbuck eyed him critically.

"You swap your horse this morning?" he demanded angrily. "One you're forking looks like he's about done in. Get over to the *remuda* and draw a fresh one."

Kent, sweaty features expressionless, wheeled about and loped toward the supply of extra mounts. Soreheads and a greenhorn, Starbuck thought bitterly, a hell of a crew to be bossing on a drive.

"There's a few things I want to say," Starbuck began that evening after the herd had been bedded down and all was quiet. "Aim to make it short because I don't want the cattle left alone."

The men faced him from the opposite side of the fire

Arkansas had built. Some hunched on their heels, while others were standing with arms folded across their chest, hats pushed back as they waited in silence for him to speak.

"We've had some bad luck but it can't last forever—"

"That's what you think maybe," Vance said in a jeering voice. "Way I see it, it ain't going to end until you—"

Anger rushed through Starbuck in a surging wave. He reacted instantly, and contrary to his usual manner, without thought. But frustration, anxiety, and the pressure of unwanted responsibility all combined to overpower better judgment in one instantaneous fraction of time.

In half a dozen long strides he was across the intervening space and confronting Vance. His right hand shot out, grasped the drover by his shirt front, and whirled him half around. His left came up in a swift curve, smashing solidly against the man's jaw and driving him to his knees.

Breathing hard, suddenly aware of what he had done, Starbuck pulled back. He looked down at Vance, now dazedly shaking his head, then to the faces of the other men watching mutely. He had made a mistake. Force was no answer, he knew that, but it was too late to remedy the situation—and apology would only further weaken his position. Fists knotted, he wheeled, dropped back to his place on the opposite side of the fire, and with jaw set, coldly returned the stares of the drovers.

"I'm tired of hearing that hogwash. Come tomorrow, after we've crossed the river we're coming to, those of you that are of a mind, can quit. Drive'll go better without you."

Shawn paused, allowing Will Vance to pull himself to his feet. "You hear that?"

Vance, head clear, glared at him with eyes burning with pure hate. "I heard. . . . You firing us?"

"No, giving you a chance to either straighten up or pull out. It's your choice."

Will glanced around, forcing a half smile. "You think you and maybe five or six hands can get three thousand head of cattle to Dodge?"

"Don't aim to try. I'm hiring on new men to replace the ones who quit."

Disbelief covered the rider's ruddy features. "Hiring—where?"

"My business," Starbuck snapped. "Now, get back on the job—those of you on the early shift, and all of you do some thinking about what I've said. You've got until we've crossed the river to make up your—"

The quick pound of boots broke into Shawn's words. He whirled. Manny was running toward them, dark face strained, eyes wide.

"*Señor caporal*—the horses!" the Mexican cried as he hurried up. "A *leon*—a big cat has scare them! They have break the *reatas* and run away!"

Nearby Starbuck heard Joe Fargo swear hoarsely. Across the fire Vance smirked, the low flames reflecting on his swarthy skin.

"All right, Manny, we'll get them back," he said to the agitated wrangler, and turned his attention again to the men. "Some of you mount up, give us some help."

Without waiting to see who complied, Shawn crossed

to where his horse was picketed and swung onto the saddle. Tally one more for Will Vance, he thought wearily.

17

The following day was a tense one for Starbuck. It would take very little in the way of an accident or unexpected incident to bring about wholesale desertion on the part of the drovers, and that, coupled with the knowledge that the bushwhacker was still about, made for a succession of uneasy hours.

But near sundown, after they had crossed the Pease River and had bedded the cattle in a convenient swale, the harsh pressures began to ease. No problems other than those considered ordinary and usual had developed. The crew had worked well, and he took a measure of reassurance from that—but he was not fooling himself; trouble lay deep, was far from over, and when the evening meal was past and the time was at hand to again declare himself, he felt tension rising within him once more.

"You still calling them to account, like you said?" Joe Fargo asked as they stood at the edge of the camp, watching those of the crew off duty spread their bedrolls.

Starbuck nodded. "Have to. If I let it pass they'll figure I'm bluffing."

"Expect you're right," the old puncher said. "Got me a hunch, howsomever, that you a-flattening Will Vance yesterday done more good than anything. Sure weren't no laying down on the job today."

"Was a fool thing to do—losing my temper. Wrong way to settle anything."

"Maybe so, but these boys savvy that kind of lingo. Every dang one of them's plenty sure now you're the boss."

"Not how I like to prove it, but it's done and there's no changing it. Next thing is to see what they're going to do."

Shawn stepped forward into the circular flare of firelight. Talk ended at once. He remained quiet for a bit, letting his glance fall successively upon each man. All of the crew were present except the five with the herd.

"Time's up. Want to know where you stand," he said crisply, and settled his eyes on the nearest, Cass Walton.

The drover stirred lazily. "I'm staying."

Starbuck, with no change of expression, shifted to the rider next. "You?"

It was Amos Green. "Me, too . . . reckon that goes for the whole bunch."

Shawn felt his spirits lift. "Glad to hear it. That includes the men with the cattle?"

"Them, too," Yeager said, speaking up. "Maybe not all of them for the same reason, but they'll stick."

"What other reason is there?"

Yeager spat into the fire. "Vance says he sure ain't letting you jockey him into getting himself in bad with Tom Zook by walking off the job. Said he'll keep working till the drive's over, no matter what."

Shawn considered the information. "He the only one looking at it that way?"

"We ain't for certain," Walton replied quickly, which

simply meant there were others who shared Vance's attitude but that no names would be forthcoming. "You willing to let it go at that?"

Starbuck shrugged. It wasn't exactly the kind of basis he'd hoped for, but he guessed it was something he could live with.

"All right with me, long as every man pulls his weight. I'm not accepting it as an excuse for laying down on the job."

Yeager glanced up from the cigarette he was rolling "I hire out to a man, I give him his money's worth. Reckon the rest of the boys feel the same."

"Was the way of it today. Can't say it goes for yesterday or the day before."

"That was yesterday," the drover observed coolly. "You won't have no call to bellyache from here on."

"Good," Shawn said, and pivoting on his heel, walked off toward the chuck wagon.

Arkansas met him with a cup of coffee. "Expect that was what you were wanting to hear."

"It was," Starbuck said, wrapping both hands around the tin container. "Only hope they mean it."

"They do. Hell, they're all good men, just got a bug in their head—mostly on account of Will Vance. You straightening him out, sort of straightened them out, too."

"I'll wait and see," Starbuck said, handing back the empty cup. "Obliged for the coffee."

The night passed without incident, and the next day, darkly overcast, presented no problems. The cattle had taken their fill of water at the Pease, grass was plentiful, and such conditions made for easy handling.

Shawn, scouting ahead with Joe Fargo, halted around mid-afternoon on a low hill and looked down upon a fairly good river that angled across the wooded country through which they were moving.

"That the Red?"

Fargo nodded. "That's it. Plenty low—and I reckon we ought to be glad of that. Can be pretty mean sometimes."

"We're lucky the rains have held off."

"For sure," Fargo said, glancing at the threatening sky, "but they ain't going to be doing that much longer. Got a feeling it's going to bust loose mighty soon, and water'll start coming down like it was being poured out of a bucket."

"Today, you think?"

"Maybe, but I'm guessing it won't be for a while yet. Could hit tomorrow, or even day after that. Clouds just don't look ready yet."

"Once we're across the river it won't matter too much. What's the country like on the other side?"

"Well, we'll be out of Texas, for one thing, and in the Indian Territory. Be a couple of days or so of dry camp, then we'll reach the Washita."

"Cattle should be in good shape for that. Can let them water good here."

The old drover glanced again to the sky. "Prob'ly have more wet than we bargain for before we hit the Washita. . . . The boys doing the job the way you're wanting?"

"No complaints. You hear any talk?"

Joe shook his head. "Vance and his crowd are all mighty close-mouthed. Sort of like they was just waiting, holding off, expecting things to bust wide open."

"Got that idea myself," Shawn said, looking back over his shoulder. The flats and the low hills were empty except for the herd, which was less than a mile distant and coming on steadily.

"Crossing the Red puts us about half way to Dodge. Quite a piece yet to go. You going to be able to put up with their foolishness that long?"

"Expect I can—and will. All I'm interested in is getting the herd delivered."

Fargo grinned. "Which I reckon you'll do come brimstone or blizzard. . . . You seen any more of that head hunter?"

"Nobody's taken a shot at me lately, if that's what you mean," Starbuck replied with grim humor.

The levity was lost on the old drover. "Which ain't no guarantee of nothing. I've been keeping my eyes peeled and I sure ain't seen nobody around. Think maybe he's give up?"

"Like to think so but I doubt it. . . . Come on, let's spot a crossing. I'll feel better once we've got the cattle on the other side of that river."

18

"There a chance we'll have trouble with Indians?"

It was Kent asking the question, and Shawn thought he detected a note of fear in the man's voice. Likely he was remembering the brush they'd had with Apaches back in the Peloncillos.

Fargo, sprawled on his bedroll near the fire, glanced around at the others taking their ease after the day's close, and winked broadly. "Won't hardly be natural if we don't."

The crossing of the Red had been an easy one, although a few steers were lost when they slipped on the uncertain footing and were overrun by those coming behind them. That was to be expected, however. All big river fordings were considered hazardous, and their deaths did not fall into the category of hard luck, which had become a descriptive term for the drive.

Having finished making an inspection of the horses in the *remuda* to assure himself that all were in good condition, Starbuck paused beside the chuck wagon before taking a turn around the herd and a check of the men watching it.

"You've made this here drive many a time, I reckon." Gabe was asking as he hacked at the corner of a plug of black tobacco with his skinning knife.

"Six, maybe seven drives now."

"You ever have Indian trouble?"

"Sure. Man looks for it through here. Last couple of years, howsomever, the soldiers sort of got them tamed down. Most of the tribes are on reservations, they claim. But I can recollect when we expected them to be waiting on the yonder side of every hump.

"Some were friendly, wanting only for us to give them a batch of steers for eating meat. With all antelope and buffalo gone, the poor beggars was plain hungry most of the time."

"Was on a drive once when a bunch stopped us and wanted twenty-five head," Amos Green said. "Claimed it was payment for crossing their land."

"They get them?"

"Yes, sir—trail boss we had knowed which end of the horse the bridle went on! Was about thirty of them, only eight of us, and they looked plenty mean. We just handed them over, nice as you please, and kept going."

"Was the wrong thing," Crawford said, shaking his head. "That kind of knuckling under made it hard on every drive that went through after that."

"Maybe so," Green said mildly, "but was I bossing that drive I'd've done the same thing. Them bucks was well armed—maybe not many rifles, but plenty of lances and bows and arrows and knives. They could've skewered us good."

"Kind of reminds me of a time we went through here, this same trail. We was this side of the Washita and Tom'd got word that the Indians was acting up something fierce. We was all keeping our eyes open. Justice had told Tom to pay off any redskins that jumped us so long as it was reasonable—fifteen, maybe twenty head.

"Well, all of a sudden we found ourselves all hemmed in by about fifty braves. The chief, I reckon it was, comes up and makes Tom savvy that they was wanting one steer apiece. Now, that was a mighty steep price. We was only droving about fifteen hundred head, so he starts arguing about it. Then another buck pipes up, speaking English good as you or me, and says we'd best do what the big cheese said and hand over the critters 'cause they'd take them away anyway and we'd better stay friendly.

"There was more hunting parties waiting along the trail he said, and they'd be wanting a slice of the pie, too, and unless we forked over the fifty they was wanting, we wouldn't get no help keeping them others off'n our back.

"Tom took it to mean they'd sort of protect us from the rest of the Indians if we paid up, so that's what we done, cutting out fifty steers and heading them off into the hills. Them braves took after them right quick and was gone, and pretty soon we begin to figure we'd been hornswoggled."

Green bobbed his head. "Plenty tricky, every dang one of them. And it sure pleasures them to pull the wool over a white man's eyes."

"Well, this bunch done right by us," Fargo continued, staring into the fire. "We moved out next morning figuring, just like you're saying, that we'd been crooked. Then pretty soon them braves started showing up—all fifty of them. Was the same bunch, I reckon. They never did get closer'n a quarter mile to us and the herd—just rode along, half of them on one side, rest on the other.

"And they stayed there clean till we got to Camp Supply. Seen other Indians along the way, but they kept their distance and didn't bother us none. Was mighty comforting, that part, but I'm telling you now, having them braves a-riding along on both sides of us for three days, and knowing they was still out there when it got dark, was enough to set the crawlers creeping up a man's backbone."

Shawn glanced at Kent. The young rider was sitting transfixed, eyes on Joe Fargo, drinking in every word the older man was speaking.

Green yawned noisily. "There's them who say if a fellow treats an Indian right, he'll get treated right hisself. I reckon it's true."

"Not for my money," Gus Yeager said flatly. "I don't trust none of them. I figure they'd as soon lift your hair as look at you."

Someone threw an armload of dry branches onto the fire, setting it to sparking and flaring into flames. In its glow the faces of the men appeared to be chiseled bronze. There was a general stirring about. Yeager dug a pipe and doeskin pouch of tobacco from a pocket and began to prepare a smoke. Crawford tipped back his head, looked up at the dark sky, and shrugged.

"Same here. I'd take my chances with a raider before I would with a redskin. Something different about fighting a white man. Guess maybe it's that you sort've know what to expect. Indians are different. Can't never figure what they're apt to do."

There was a pause after that. Amos Green rose, shambled to the smaller fire near the shuttler, and poured himself a cup of coffee from the blackened pot simmering on the coals. He looked at Shawn as he passed, his glance neither friendly nor hostile, merely noncommittal.

"What about them raiders?" someone asked. "Anybody heard if they're running loose this year?"

"Run loose every year," Fargo said. "If we don't get jumped before we hit the Arkansas, I'll be a mighty surprised gander. Far as I'm concerned they're bad as the Comanches—worse even."

"That's gospel for sure," Green said, resuming his place. "Unless it's a war party looking to blood themselves, a man can usually do some palavering with Indians, swap them out of their meanness. Can't do that with them raiders. They know what they want and go after it. Killing another white man don't count for nothing with them."

Starbuck drew away from the wagon against which he was leaning and glanced at the sky. It was a solid black canopy, unbroken anywhere by moon or stars. The coolness in the air strengthened his belief that rain was not far off. He turned, moving toward the horses. This was the way a camp should be—the drovers taking their ease around a fire, talking, telling of the past, recounting their experiences.

"You think we may have to fight some of those raiders?" It was Kent again.

"Sure won't be no surprise if we do," Fargo answered. "If we're lucky we won't."

"Which we ain't," Crawford said in a gusty voice. "So best get yourself set for some hard shooting."

Irritation quickened Shawn's pulse, overriding the satisfaction he had felt as he swung onto the buckskin Manny had brought up for him. The men were still unconvinced. They were going along with him, doing their job, but still with the belief the drive was jinxed and that he was a Jonah.

There was nothing he could do about it, however, except, as he'd told Fargo, live with it and hope that something would not occur to further support their conviction. That it would was certainly possible, he realized as he rode out of camp; a bushwhacker could look for no better opportunity than this dark night to try his hand again.

Joe Fargo watched carefully as Starbuck mounted his

horse and quietly left the camp. Shawn would be going to make his ride around the herd, satisfy himself that the men doing nighthawk were awake and on the job. He trusted none of them, took nothing for granted, although every drover on that particular shift was an experienced, reliable man. But he reckoned they'd all given their trail boss good reason to mistrust them.

Pulling himself to a sitting position, Fargo yawned, glancing around at the riders sprawled on their blankets. Some were dozing, others were simply staring into the fire. Kent rose, moving off into the darkness below the wagon. Crawford roused also and crossed to the chuck wagon for a final cup of coffee.

Yawning again, Joe Fargo got to his feet. "Reckon I'll stretch my legs a mite before turning in," he said to no one in particular, and strolled away from the fire's glow.

Once beyond the light he quickly circled, and unseen, returned to the camp just below the rope corral where Manny had the remounts picketed. Halting there he looked about until he located the wrangler rolled up in his blanket under the chuck wagon, sleeping soundly. Fargo then continued on to where half a dozen saddled and bridled horses, awaiting the second shift of night herders, were tethered.

Taking the first, he cut back into the dark night and rode on, following a course he figured Starbuck would have taken. The night was black, and visibility was poor, something he supposed Shawn had given thought to but had chosen to ignore. He was that way, Fargo had discovered; the fact that conditions made for personal danger was not cause for him to neglect what he believed was his job.

A low growl of thunder in the east brought the old man to a halt, stroking his mustache he contemplated the void that was the sky. The storm would break sooner than he had thought; it was good the Red was behind them. It could be tricky when the water was high.

Off to the left the soft thunk of a walking horse drew his immediate attention. Leaning forward he squinted, trying to pierce the darkness with his eyes.

"Shawn?" he called.

The hoof beats ceased instantly. Fargo waited a long minute, and then touching his horse lightly with his heels, moved forward quietly. The herd was still some distance farther on, and he doubted it would be one of the drovers; besides, if it was one of them, his query would have brought a response, the same as it would if it were Starbuck.

Suddenly suspicious, Fargo drew his pistol. He continued, holding his mount to a slow walk, eyes and ears alert. Unexpectedly, from the opposite side, the creak of leather came to him. He wheeled as a figure loomed up in the murk.

"Hold it right there!" he barked. "Who is it?"

"Me—Starbuck."

At Shawn's voice the older man relaxed. "Figured you was with the herd."

"Had a look. Everything's fine," Starbuck said. "Not sure it'll stay that way if this storm cuts loose."

"Going to hit before sun up. You see anybody else riding along here?"

"Nobody—only you. Why?"

"Heard a horse walking. Sung out but got no answer. Figured it was you at first."

"I wasn't this far over, except for now. Could've been a stray—or maybe a deer."

"Reckon so," Fargo grunted, making no issue of what he knew. "You done riding around in the dark?"

"For a while."

"All right, then. Let's head back to camp and grab a little shut-eye. My turn's coming up in a few hours and I'm knowing you're needing some rest."

"Won't argue that," Shawn said, and moved on.

Joe Fargo kneed his horse in beside him. He wasn't buying Starbuck's explanation, not for a moment; there had been someone prowling the night—someone who was careful to preserve his identity. . . . And the only man with that in mind had to be the bushwhacker. . . . It was a good thing he'd taken a notion to follow Shawn.

19

The rain, cold and steady, came shortly after sunrise. Arkansas, expecting it, had stretched a tarp from the top of the wagon, and anchoring its corners to nearby clumps of rabbitbush, he managed to provide a dry, hot breakfast for the riders.

There was a minimum amount of thunder and lightning, neither of which seemed to disturb the cattle to any extent. They moved out with little more than the usual amount of effort on the part of the drovers. But as the day wore on and the storm continued, alternating between drizzles and sudden flurries of stinging, pelting drops, the land over which they traveled turned slowly into a slippery sea of churned mud.

Camp that night was a miserable affair saved only by the fact that Arkansas had thoughtfully stored a quantity of dry wood inside the shuttler as a precaution against just such an occasion and thus was able to again come up with a good meal.

The rain continued its persistent attack throughout the night and the following day. The cook's dry-wood supply ran out, and Shawn delegated two of the drovers to assist him in searching the hills for branches, dead roots and the like that could be found under rocks and thick brush.

Conditions became increasingly hazardous as the storm failed to slacken. Around noon of the third slate-gray day, with the stinging drops still pouring down from an unfriendly sky with slashing force, the cattle came to a stop of their own accord and stubbornly refused to continue. Starbuck called a halt to all efforts to move them, deciding it was just as well they break for the night and hope the storm would fade before morning.

Making use of boxes and other combustible items in the chuck wagon, Arkansas got a fire going under his tarp and produced a supper of sorts, discovering, incidentally, a quart bottle of whiskey in his personal effects, which he passed around. The liquor served to raise the sodden spirits of the drovers to some degree, but when the long, cold night was over and the heavens were still low and filled with rain, the general air of depression set in once more.

Late in the morning, as the herd slogged along at a snail's pace under the indifferent attention of the water-soaked riders, the chuck wagon, despite Arkansas' efforts, slid down the slope of a slight hill and over-turned, spilling about half its contents onto the muddy ground.

Shawn, calling in most of the crew to assist, worked with the cook to right the vehicle and recover its con-tents. Most of the dry foods were lost, but on the whole not too much damage was done except to morale.

Standing in the steady downpour while he scraped the slick, clinging clay from his boots and the front of his slicker, Starbuck looked up to see Cass Walton and the man called Eli walk to the wagon and paw among the sodden blanket rolls until they found their own. Then together they crossed to their horses and began tying the gear to their saddles. Nearby, Will Vance, ready to mount and return to the herd with some of the other men, paused.

"You boys pulling out?"

Walton bobbed his head angrily. "Just as fast, by God, as we can! I'm plumb up to my Adam's apple with this sonofabitching drive—and so's Eli. Ain't nothing but bad luck. We're streaking it for the closest town where a man can dry off and get hisself a decent meal."

"Can't say as I blame you," Vance said, and glanced slyly at Shawn. "Appears you're a couple more drovers short, Mister Trail Boss. I'm starting to wonder if we'll ever make it to Dodge."

"We'll make it," Starbuck said quietly, and turned to the two men now swinging onto their saddles. "Anything I can say that'll change your mind?"

Eli looked down. Cass Walton shrugged. "Nothing.

Just can't put up with this no longer."

"You've been on drives before where there were accidents—and it rained."

"Not like this'n. I'm plenty sorry to quit on you, but I ain't young as I used to be, and this here's just got to be too much. . . . Tell Tom Zook I'll drop by and see him some day. He can either pay me off or run me off, whichever he's of a notion. So long."

Abruptly the pair wheeled about and headed across the water-covered flat that lay to the east. Sober, Shawn stepped back under the canvas canopy Arkansas had now erected. He was four men short now—five if you counted Zook—and he had to admit that the prospects for getting Morgan Justice's herd to Dodge City were steadily growing smaller.

"Was you listening to suggestions," Ligon said, chafing his wet hands vigorously, "I'd say it'd be smart to drive the cattle up into the hills and then go hunting for some help."

"And let the Indians help themselves?" Fargo demanded before Shawn could reply. "Quick as this rain's over they'll be swarming all through here, hungry as a grizzly in the spring. We'd lose half the herd."

"Better'n losing it all," Vance observed. "Said it before and I'll say it again, a hard-luck drive like this'll never get through. Just ain't in the cards." He paused, looking around at the men huddled beneath the tarp. "What say we take us a vote on whether to leave the herd here, like Ligon says?"

"You don't," Starbuck said flatly. "We move on in the morning, same as usual."

The corners of Vance's mouth pulled down into a hard grin. "You scared to let us vote on it?"

"Makes no difference to me, one way or the other. It won't change anything."

"But if we—"

"You and the rest of the crew aren't bossing this drive—I am, and I'll make the decisions. If you don't like it, then pick up your gear and follow Eli and Cass."

Vance continued to grin, but the grimace was more frozen than confident. He settled his eyes on Kent.

"What about you, boy? You want to keep working wet as a dog, eating nothing but soggy grub that ain't fit for nothing but hogs—and waiting for something bad to happen to you? That what all the rest of you want?"

Charlie Hubbard reached up, pulled his hat lower on his head. "Hell, I been wet before—and hungry, too. Come on, lets get to the herd so's the rest of the boys can come in and dry off. . . . Arky, I'll drop back soon as I can and help you rustle up some wood."

Moving out from under the canvas cover, the squat drover strode to where his horse waited, brushed futilely at the rain-soaked seat of his saddle, and stepped up, swearing softly as he settled himself. Kent and two others followed at once, and then the rest, including Will Vance, started for their mounts.

Joe Fargo grinned wryly at Shawn. "Figured for a bit there that it was going to be me and you and Arkansas, and maybe the Mex, winding up this drive."

"Could turn out that way yet," Starbuck said grimly as he headed toward his horse.

20

The rain ceased that next day, but not until another accident was added to the slowly mounting score. The horse Amos Green was riding fell on a slippery slope, broke two of its legs, and had to be destroyed. Fortunately, Green suffered only a badly wrenched back.

Shawn, determined to complete the drive, pushed the vast herd on doggedly. Constantly aware of his own personal danger, he was watchful and reserved. They reached the Washita River, camped there for a night and pressed on to the Canadian, the cattle at last trailing well over the spongy, cool land.

"Luck sure ain't all bad," Joe Fargo remarked the night before they were due to arrive at Camp Supply, near the Kansas border. "We ain't had no Kiowa or Comanche visitors."

"Reckon we can thank the bad weather for that," Hubbard said.

Starbuck had no comment. They were still in Indian country and he'd delay such congratulations until all possible danger was past. Cattle losses had been amazingly small despite the problems encountered—something less than fifty head, he thought, and he was hopeful of losing no more. Chances that they wouldn't were good; the greater portion of the trail was behind them, but he would wait.

Two days later they reached Camp Supply and bedded the herd on a flat near the north fork of the Canadian, just beyond. Leaving Joe Fargo in charge, Shawn and

Arkansas rode in the shuttler to the army establishment—the cook to replenish his stock of groceries, Starbuck to see if he could hire on riders to replace the four no longer with him.

He was able to sign up two men, Texans on their way back home from another drive and tarrying at the post for a few days of relaxation. Sending them out to the herd at once with instructions to report to Fargo, he then sought the commanding officer of the camp, a Major Taft.

"Name's Starbuck," he said as he entered the military man's office. "Got a herd bedded down north of here. On my way to Dodge City."

Taft, a tall, angular man well up in years, rose from his chair and extended a hand. "It's been reported," he said, nodding. "Large herd, so I'm told."

"Left Texas with three thousand head. I've managed to get this far with most of them."

"No trouble from the Indians?"

"Not so far. Had bad weather across most of the territory. Expect that helped."

The officer smiled, settling back in his chair. "Probably. If you can get by the Tonkawas now without any problems, you'll be doing all right."

"Tonkawas? Thought they were friendly."

"Are, but they've got a notion that the herds of cattle coming into Kansas are to replace the buffalo the white men killed off and are forever helping themselves. There's an old saying around here that cattlemen lose more stock to the friendly Tonkawas than they do to the hostile Cheyennes and Comanches. "

"Hadn't heard about them."

"Well, be prepared to lose a few head—all for the sake of peace."

Starbuck grinned. "I'll be ready. One thing I was figuring to ask about is the outlaw situation across the line. Been told the raiders are sometimes pretty bad. There any report of them lately?"

"Some. Out of my area, of course, but we do get word now and then. Most recent was a week or so ago. A large band hit a herd being driven into Dodge. Were several men killed and quite a number of cattle driven off."

"Isn't the army able to do something about it?"

"We try," Taft said, assuming the patience accorded civilians by the military. "Troopers have been sent in from Fort Hays—even as far east as Gibson—in an effort to clean them out, but they've always disappeared before they could be engaged." The officer paused, drumming on his desk with his fingertips. "For the time being, a man crossing that part of Kansas is pretty much on his own. We can't manage to be everywhere."

"No point then in asking for an escort?"

"Absolutely none. Have my hands full keeping things in order here. The garrison's undermanned. Never enough to do a proper job."

"I see—"

"Only suggestion I can make is that you go in well armed and on full alert until you reach the Arkansas. With a herd large as yours you undoubtedly have quite a few men. That could make them leave you alone. However, if you do run into trouble, and it's close to the border, send word and I'll try to get a patrol there in time to help."

Starbuck offered his hand. "Obliged to you, Major," he said, and hesitated. "One thing more, I hired on two drovers who say they've been here for a few days. You happen to know if that's the truth?"

"It's my business to know," Taft said crisply. "They have—for about a week."

A buck sergeant entered the office, saluted, laid a sheaf of papers on the desk, saluted again, and retreated.

"Anybody else pass through today, or perhaps yesterday? A man by himself?"

Taft, fingering the papers, looked up, shook his head. "You and your cook are the only ones for the past week. And those two Texans, of course. You expecting to meet somebody?"

To tell the officer about the bushwhacker would be meaningless, and it was evident he had stayed clear of the post. Starbuck smiled, turning toward the door. "No, just wondering if there was anyone else around," he said, and returned to the yard.

Arkansas had completed his purchasing and was leaning against the wagon in conversation with a soldier. Shawn rejoined the cook, and climbing onto the seat of the shuttler, they pulled out of the camp and struck north for the herd.

"Able to get all you were short of?" Shawn asked when they were well underway.

"Nearabouts," Arkansas replied, passing him the change from the money advanced. "Reckon I can satisfy some bellies tonight. You have any luck hiring drovers?"

"Couple of Texans. Told them to report to Joe."

"That'll help a-plenty—if they showed up."

The pair had, and Fargo immediately put them to work. The crew, Starbuck found, was in a much better frame of mind, and their spirits improved even more after the big, evening meal prepared by Arkansas was made ready. It seemed to him, as the evening wore on, that there had been a change in their outlook, also, that the tension had decreased and they were less apprehensive about the miles that still lay ahead.

This mood prevailed the next morning when they moved out, and Shawn felt his own optimism rising. He purposely delayed mentioning Taft's cautioning words concerning the raiders, not wanting to dampen the men's spirits. He intended to make known the officer's warning when they were ready to depart the following day.

But at sundown, when they halted for night camp not far from the Kansas line, it became apparent the tenor of the drover's attitudes had altered again. Once more glum and withdrawn, those not with the herd gathered around the fire after supper was over, and almost at once Gus Yeager approached him, his tone faintly, accusing.

"Hinson and Buttram, them new fellows you hired've been telling us about the raiders. Claim things are plenty bad right now. You know anything about it?"

Starbuck shrugged. He should have guessed the pair would pass along the word of what could be expected. His efforts to maintain an aura of cheerfulness had gone for nothing.

"The major at the camp said they'd hit a herd about a week ago. Could be that'll satisfy them for a spell."

"He figure it will?"

"My idea, not his. All we can do is be ready. I want

every man armed from here on—pistol and rifle."

Will Vance groaned. "Reckon we know now what to expect."

"You ain't much at looking at the bright side!" Fargo said sourly. "Ain't no for-sure we'll get jumped. Starbuck could be right."

"He ain't done so good so far," Vance replied, and then added quickly, "not that he ain't done some real hard trying. Just that we ain't got no luck."

"Still driving most of the steers we headed out with— and that's something."

Vance brushed that off with a wave of his hand. "With one man dead and buried, and a whole passel of hard luck to go with that, I ain't so certain it counts for much. And now with us riding straight into a bunch of jayhawk killers, I figure we—"

"Wait till tomorrow," Fargo cut in, "then do your dooms-daying if it's needful. I got a hunch we're going to sail right on into Dodge without a hitch."

But Joe Fargo's prediction fell short. Near mid-afternoon of the second day in Kansas the raiders struck.

21

The first indication of an attack was a sudden, furious burst of gunshots. They came from the west, the left flank of the herd, and somewhere near the front.

Starbuck riding drag, with Hubbard, Fargo, and Kent close by, immediately spurred toward the sound of the disturbance. Half way he slowed. The area on that side of the trail was mainly flat ground. Why would the outlaws, bent on driving off a portion of the cattle, choose such open country, when to the east lay a maze of hills and broken land into which they could quickly disappear? There could only be one answer. Wheeling the sorrel about he doubled back to the others.

"It's a trick!" he shouted as he drew in close. "They're trying to draw us off! Charlie, you and Kent stay put— keep after the stragglers! Joe—come with me!"

Immediately he cut across to the right flank of the herd, and with Fargo pounding alongside, raced toward its front. Gunshots were now a continuing rattle echoing above the thudding of the hooves, coming from point as well as the opposite side.

"There they are!" Fargo yelled, dragging out his pistol.

Starbuck saw them at the same moment. Six or eight men—he couldn't be sure in the haze—crowding into the cattle, already carving out a portion of two hundred head or so. He'd been right; the shooting on the west flank had been designed to attract the drovers, leaving the east unprotected.

The plan had worked insofar as his riders were concerned. There was no one in sight except the raiders. The men had been attracted by the shots and had already gone to the aid of their friends. Shawn turned to face Fargo, raised a restraining hand.

"Hold up—"

Frowning, the old rider pulled to a halt beside him. "Ain't you going to stop them?"

"Too big a job for just us—we'd lose the cattle for sure," Shawn answered. "Want you to drop back around, get about a half a dozen men—no more than that—and bring them here. The others had best stay with the herd. The shooting's got it running and it could start splitting up."

Fargo nodded his understanding. "Where'll you be?"

"Right along here somewheres, keeping that bunch in sight."

Joe Fargo whirled away, and Starbuck, eyes on the raiders, loped on, staying close to the cattle where he figured he would not be noticed.

The outlaws had cut out their jag of steers and were swinging them away from the main body. There were eight men in all, now clear in the dust pall raised from the churned land which apparently had not enjoyed the heavy rains visited upon the country farther south. Instead of using their guns, they were hazing the steers with ropes and waved hats, thus avoiding attracting the drovers engaged in exchanging shots with the remainder of the gang on the west side.

Within only a few minutes they had the stock clear and running for the short hills. Shawn, anxious, glanced over his shoulder. Time enough had elapsed for Fargo to— At that moment he saw the older man, with several drovers bunched close behind, break out of the pall and come toward him.

Relieved, he roweled the sorrel and sent the big gelding plunging ahead in the wake of the raiders and the cattle they were driving. He heard a shout and knew that Fargo and the others had spotted him and were pressing hard to catch up.

Holding back his horse to allow them to draw abreast, he glanced over the men: Yeager . . . Cal Ligon . . . Kent

. . . Amos Green . . . Chesson . . . Will Vance. He frowned. Kent, raw and inexperienced, was a poor choice to be facing outlaw guns. The same went for Vance—for a different reason. But there was no making any changes now.

"Charlie said he'd see to the herd," Fargo yelled as they moved together. "Said he'd run them clean on till they hit the Arkansas!"

Shawn nodded. "Split up!" he shouted back. "Half move in on the left, rest on the right. They haven't seen us yet!"

Fargo raised his hand and divided the force. "Somebody ought to get out ahead, try turning them critters! They get to them hills, they'll scatter from hell to breakfast!"

"What I'll try to do once they've seen us and drop back to make a fight of it."

Gunshots echoed his words. Two of the outlaws at the rear of the small herd had become aware of their presence and were opening up.

"Reckon now's the time!" Fargo yelled, and with a sweep of his arm sent Ligon, Vance, and Yeager veering off to the right, the others to the left.

"I'm riding with you!" he shouted to Shawn. "Let's go!"

The old rider didn't wait to hear Starbuck's objections. Driving his spurs into the flanks of the horse he was riding, he rushed on ahead at a faster gallop, triggering his weapon as he went.

Shawn cut in beside him, and on the faster sorrel, forged past, cutting across behind the men on the right and bearing directly at the outlaws as they fired. A rider broke away from the front of the cattle, drawn from that point by the shooting. Pulling up short, he drew his pistol.

Starbuck, steadying his aim, pressed off a shot. The outlaw flinched, then fired. Shawn, more careful now, squeezed the trigger of his forty-five again. The man sagged, then fell from his shying horse.

"That there's one jayhawker that won't be bothering nobody from now on!" Fargo yelled, and resting his pistol upon his left forearm, triggered his weapon twice in quick succession.

"There's another'n!" he added.

Shawn glanced toward the drovers. They were swerving more sharply left now, pulling away from the running cattle. The raiders were giving up, falling back, hopeful, no doubt, of rejoining the rest of their party. He saw a riderless horse suddenly come into view at the far edge of the herd, and quickly wondered if it belonged to one of his drovers or to one of the outlaws, then gave it no more thought as he pulled up beside the lead steers in the madly running bunch.

Cutting in close, he dragged off his hat and began to slap at the wild-eyed animal nearest to him, shouting his loudest as he did. A moment later Fargo joined him and added his efforts.

Slowly the cattle began to turn, checked as gunshots erupted along their left flank. The two men increased their pressure, now making use of their guns. The steers gave ground once more and abruptly veered. Beyond them, Starbuck caught sight of his men—three of them in hot pursuit of two raiders streaking for the hills to the northeast.

"We got them going!" Fargo cried.

The dry slap of a bullet as it smashed into his saddle brought Starbuck up sharply. He had thought all of the outlaws were on the opposite side of the cattle. Evidently he had been wrong. Cutting the sorrel hard right, he rodded the empties from the cylinder of his pistol and thumbed in fresh loads.

A second bullet plucked at his sleeve. He ducked low as Fargo turned to stare at him, and he threw his glance to the thin roll of dust trailing the steers. He could see no rider, but someone was certainly taking advantage of the screening pall.

"I'll get him!" Fargo said as he spurred by. "You look to them steers!"

"No—" Shawn yelled, endeavoring to stop the drover, but Fargo raced on, hunched low over his saddle, pistol ready.

Turning back, Starbuck gave his attention to the herd. Far over to the right he could see two riders loping back toward him, evidently having driven the outlaws they were chasing into the hills. There had been three men when he first noticed them. He wondered about the missing man. Other drovers were coming in on the left, their objectives also apparently accomplished.

Having spotted the main herd in the near distance, the cattle began to increase their gait. They would require little attention now. Anxious to rejoin their own kind, they would continue of their own accord.

Starbuck slowed as Ligon and Yeager rode up. Both were smiling. "Winged one of them," the latter said.

"And there's a couple more down. Expect it was you or Joe got them."

Shawn nodded. "Who was that with you?"

"Amos—for a spell. He cut off, went chasing after another'n. Don't see Joe."

"Cut back when somebody started shooting at us from behind," Starbuck replied, holding up a frayed jacket sleeve and looking down at the cantle of his saddle, in which a bullet had buried itself.

"Close," Ligon murmured, frowning. "You reckon Amos got his?"

Yeager shook his head, turning half around as several riders came into view. "He ain't with them—and they got somebody hanging across a saddle."

It was Fargo with Kent, Vance, and Roy Chesson. Shawn felt a heaviness settle into his heart; another man lost—and there could be more. He had yet to hear from the ones who had fought it out with the outlaws on the other side of the herd. Fargo's features were solemn as he drew up.

"That Amos?" Yeager asked quietly.

The old puncher's shoulders stirred. "It's him. Reckon Arkansas'll be making another cross."

"Goddam them jayhawker bastards," Yeager said softly. "Should've kept running them till we knocked them clean off their saddles."

"I figure it could've been the one that was taking them potshots at you," Fargo said to Shawn as they swung about and moved toward the herd. "Weren't no sign of him when I got there. Seen me coming, I expect, and high-tailed it to join up with his friends over on the other side."

Starbuck was silent for a time. Then, "About the way of it," he said, but the thought lodged in his mind was far different. Could it have been the bushwhacker taking advantage of the moment to try his luck again? If so, he had come uncomfortably close to succeeding.

22

Hubbard had brought the herd to a halt on the banks of the Arkansas, reluctant to attempt a crossing until the rest of the crew had caught up. Since there was still plenty of daylight remaining when Starbuck and the rest arrived, they proceeded with the fording, and by the time darkness fell, the cattle were on the opposite side and bedding down quietly.

As camp was being set up and the night watches established, he took stock of their casualties: one man dead from a raider's bullet; three wounded, none seriously; two horses shot; one steer killed, probably by a stray bullet. It could have been worse, Fargo pointed out to Shawn, but Will Vance saw it otherwise.

"Running in to bad luck right up to the last mile," he said slyly. "What do you reckon'll happen next?"

"Nothing—plain nothing," the old drover retorted. "Hell, we're same as in Dodge."

"There's still time," Will said, and moved on.

They buried Amos Green under an oak tree not far from the river, commemorating the moment with a brief service by Arkansas and erecting the second cross that he had been required to make. Afterward, silent and withdrawn, they ate the evening meal and settled down for the last night they would be spending on the trail before reaching their destination.

Curiously, unlike the death of Sim Roberson, that of Amos Green was deeply affecting most of the men. Sim had gone to glory in a stand-up shoot out, facing his killer. Green had met his end at the hands of the raiders, victim of a bullet fired by a member of the outlaw bunch. Thus there was a distinction—a very fine line, but nevertheless important. While the killing of Roberson ended with the encounter itself, that of Amos cried for vengeance, and each of his friends felt the need to do something about it.

But that would come later, Starbuck knew; they would see the drive through to its finish, and then perhaps in pairs or small groups they would return to the hilly country beyond the Arkansas and there seek out the men responsible and square accounts for Amos Green.

Realizing the frame of mind most would be in when they reached the settlement, Shawn took a moment to caution them. "Want to warn you," he said, "if you haven't been in Dodge lately you'll find it some changed. The law's tough, especially on trail hands up from Texas."

Chesson, sprawled on his blankets, looked up. "Ain't nothing new about that. Was that way before."

"Could be worse now. Got a deputy marshal by the name of Earp running things. When you hit town, check your gun at the first saloon—or leave it in your saddlebags. If you aim to do any hell-raising, stay south of the railroad tracks."

There was a long silence, broken finally by Cal Ligon.

"Don't reckon we'll be hanging around for much more'n it takes to get paid off."

"We drawing our money when we get there?" Gabe asked.

"Soon as the cattle are in the pens and the deal is closed. Zook told me to get whatever cash I need from the buyer to pay everybody off."

"About what time will that be?" Kent wanted to know.

Starbuck glanced at Fargo. "Expect you can answer that better'n me."

The drover scratched at his jaw. "Oh, I reckon we ought to have the whole kit and caboodle over and done with by dark, maybe a bit before."

"We plan to head back day after tomorrow," Shawn continued. "Aim to sell off the horses here if I can. If there's no market, we take them along. Meeting place will be right here, this same spot. Be here by sundown if you figure to go with us. We'll move out that next morning."

"Like to know who all there'll be," Arkansas said, pausing at his chores. "Going to have to lay in some grub."

Ligon glanced around. "Be about everybody, I guess, leastwise starting. Could be some'll be leaving for a spell."

"Figured that," the cook murmured, and resumed his work.

Shawn turned away, heading toward the horses. A moment later he became aware of company and looked back. It was Fargo.

"You taking a look at the herd?"

Starbuck nodded. "Too close to being finished now to let something go wrong."

"Guess I'll just tag along. Like you said, I sure would hate to see something happen now."

Shawn paused, something in the old drover's tone arresting him. "Meaning what?"

"Just this—them two shots coming at you while we was chasing them raiders didn't come from one of them, and you know it. It was that jasper that's after your hide."

Far down the river a coyote yapped into the night. Starbuck listened for a time, then finally nodded. "Seemed that way to me."

"He's been trailing along with us from the beginning, looking for chances to nail you. Found them, too, and only his poor shooting's saved your neck—but one of these here times he's bound to have some luck—"

"No doubt, but I'm hoping mine holds until I get this herd off my hands, then I'm hunting down whoever it is and do some settling. Not about to let things run on like they have."

"It's been kind of like fighting with one hand tied behind your back—which is why I'm sticking close till you get all squared up. Walking around Dodge, you're going to be needing somebody watching your tail."

Frowning, Shawn studied the older man. "You don't owe me anything, Joe. Can't see why you want to keep sticking out your neck."

Fargo's thin shoulders stirred. "One of them personal things. Aim to talk about it later." He looked up suddenly. "You ain't minding, are you?"

"Not a bit—appreciate it, in fact. It's just that I was

brought up to handle my own problems."

"Can see you were, but this here's one time I figure you can use some help. You're going to be right busy in Dodge, and there ain't no sense making it easy for that drygulcher."

"I'll agree with that," Shawn said grimly. "Come on, let's take a turn around the herd and then get some sleep. Tomorrow's going to be a long day."

By five o'clock the cattle were in the loading pens, and Starbuck had completed the transaction with Morgan Justice's buyer, drawing enough cash to pay off the drovers and arranging for the balance to be forwarded by draft to the rancher's bank. The market for horses was as usual glutted, and he sent word by Arkansas that the *remuda* would be driven back to Texas and that the wrangler was to hold the animals where they were.

When it was all done, and the men had ridden off, headed for that part of town where they could celebrate the end of the drive in whatever fashion they chose, Shawn heaved a deep sigh of relief. He had gotten the herd through, now he could look to his own problems.

"Expect you'll be wanting first to clean up and have yourself a good supper," Fargo said as they turned toward the street.

"That, and paying a call on those folks you figure might help me find my brother."

"Easy. Can do it all at the same time. Abe Glover—he's the one runs that mail thing—has got hisself a rooming house. Can put up there—do our eating, sleeping, and talking all under the same roof."

"Fine. Like to—"

"Starbuck!"

At the harsh call coming from behind them, Shawn stiffened. The muscles of his long body went taut as the thought, *the bushwhacker,* flashed through his mind. He brought the sorrel to a stop, realizing as he did, that he was in a bad way—unarmed. His pistol was off and inside his saddlebags. Surprise rocked him in that next moment as Fargo's startled voice came to him.

"Will Vance—what the hell you—"

"Stay out of this, Joe," the drover said coldly. "And you—Starbuck—climb down off that horse and hang on your iron."

Complying slowly, Shawn faced Vance. "What's this all about?"

"Ain't no need asking me that," the husky puncher replied. "Nobody rousts me about. Get your gun!"

In the half-dark deserted area near the loading pens there was only the muted sounds of the restless cattle. Starbuck shook his head.

"We're not having a shooting over that."

"Get your gun," Vance repeated. "Else I'll—"

"What's the matter with you, Will—you gone loco or something?" Fargo cut in. "Ain't no call for you—"

"Got plenty of reason. This here hoodoo thinks he's big shakes, but I aim to—"

"You ain't doing nothing, mister," a voice broke in from the shadows near the corner. "I got a Henry pointed at your middle. Make a move for that pistol you're wearing and I'll blow you apart!"

Vance froze. Starbuck turned slightly and saw a tall,

lean man wearing a star, a rifle in his hands, move into the open. He crossed to the drover in slow, careful steps, finger ready on the trigger of his weapon.

"You goddam Texicans figure you can do anything you please when you come here," he said, jerking Vance's pistol from its holster. "One of these days you're going to learn different."

The lawman drew back a step, swept Starbuck and Fargo with a critical glance. "Damn good thing you ain't armed, else I'd be locking you up, too. Now, I don't know what this is all about, but if you want to do some talking, follow me to the jail and you can tell it to Earp."

"Far as I'm concerned, forget it," Starbuck said.

The deputy bobbed his head. "I can forget your part of it, but sure'n hell ain't forgetting his," he snapped, and jabbed Vance with the muzzle of his rifle. "Start walking, Texican!"

Shawn watched the pair move off in silence, and then coming around, swung back onto the sorrel.

Joe Fargo swore. "That Will—can't figure what got into him!"

"Whiskey," Starbuck said. "Got himself a few drinks and started feeling sorry for himself. We'll get him out in the morning after he's cooled off."

"Might be smarter to just leave him there," Fargo said as they moved on.

Shawn made no comment as he reached up and brushed at the sweat on his forehead. He had known a few tight moments there in the half light before Fargo's words had told him who it was calling him out. He was almost sorry that it hadn't been the bushwhacker; the question of who it was that wanted to kill him—and why—would have been answered by now.

"That's Abe's place—house there on the corner," Fargo said, pointing ahead.

Starbuck slanted the gelding toward the hitchrack standing at the side of the two-storied structure. Lights were burning inside, turning the windows into yellow squares, and coming from somewhere nearby was the sound of music. A saloon, he thought, glancing along the darkened buildings that lined the street. A drink would go good at that moment. Will Vance had kind of set his nerves on edge.

"Hey—Abe!"

Shawn jumped a little at the drover's unexpected hail. Grinning tightly, he brought the sorrel to a halt at the rack and swung down. Somewhere over near the center of town a lone gunshot flatted hollowly.

"Abe—Abe Glover—you in there?"

A man appeared in the doorway of the house. Shading his eyes from a lamp, he peered into the gloom.

"It's me—Joe Fargo! Me and a friend that's wanting to meet you. Name's Starbuck."

Glover advanced onto the porch, a short, paunchy individual with a brushy mustache and a full beard.

"Joe, that you for certain?"

"It sure'n hell is," Fargo replied in an easy tone as he and Shawn crossed the yard to the steps that led up to the narrow veranda. "How you been?"

"Tolerable. Come in with a herd?"

"Yeh, another'n for Morgan Justice."

"Where's Zook? Generally with you."

The drover paused midway up the steps. "Tom got his-self hurt," he explained. "Starbuck here took over the bossing job." He turned to drop a hand on Shawn's shoulder and then suddenly lunged against the tall rider.

"Look out!" he yelled.

A pistol cracked the warm hush. Starbuck caught the flash of powder farther down the street from the tail of his eye as he felt Fargo's body jolt and start to fall. Reaching out quickly, he caught the drover around the waist, and lowered him gently to the steps. Nearby Glover was yelling something at him. Other voices were shouting questions.

Starbuck, ignoring all, looked closely into Fargo's lax features. The old puncher had deliberately stepped in front of him, taking the bullet undoubtedly meant for him.

"Joe—"

The drover opened his eyes and managed a half grin. "Reckon I won't be—going back—with you . . . Asking—a favor. Tell Jenny—Miz Justice—I'm mighty—sorry. She'll know what I—"

The words faded as the slight figure went limp. Shawn continued to study the man's slack features for a moment, and then removing his arms, drew himself upright. Touching Glover with a cold glance, he said, "Take care of him," and turned back down the steps.

Crossing to the sorrel, he opened his saddlebags and took out his pistol. Checking the cylinder for loads, he slid it into the holster, and stepping into the street, started toward its upper end where he had seen the powder flash. He had double reason now for settling with the bush-whacker.

23

"Down there—by that shed—"

Starbuck gave no indication that he heard the man standing in a darkened doorway as he strode toward the end of the street. His mind was filled with but one thought: at last he was going to come face to face with the bushwhacker that had been dogging his tracks, and who, in a final effort to kill him, had brought death instead to a fine old man—a good friend.

He was vaguely aware of onlookers as he moved relentlessly on at a slow, measured pace, eyes straight ahead, alert for the slightest sound that would reveal the killer's exact position. The man, whoever he was, could have fled; he had done so before after failing in an attempt, and there was no good reason to believe he would not again. Starbuck shook off the possibility, a conviction within assuring him that he was still there, that this was the final confrontation.

"Somebody ought to call the law." It was a woman's hushed voice coming from the shadows.

"They'll be showing up," the deeper tones of a man promised. "That shot was heard for sure."

"Be too late—"

"Always is at a time like this."

Wholly intent, Starbuck was barely conscious of the words being spoken. The corner where the bushwhacker had been standing was directly before him, lighted partly by lamps shining through the windows of a nearby house. He slowed, hand dropping to the butt of the forty-five slung low on his left thigh.

Off to the side a dog, aroused by his deliberate passage, began to bark furiously. A man swore. There was a dull thump, and the animal yelped in pain and fell silent. Not distracted, Shawn continued, drifting out of the pale glow, taking advantage of the cover provided by the semi-darkness along the wall of an adjacent building. He halted abruptly. His change of course had evoked movement at the corner of the shed. Cool, nerves drawn to a fine point, he waited.

"I'm here," he said, finally.

There was a faint scuffing in the shadows. Back up the street a short distance, several men had come into the open and were watching with avid interest.

"Step out where I can see you—or do you aim to keep on hiding like you've been doing ever since Arizona?"

Silence was Starbuck's only answer. He rode out another long minute, then, "Been your way all along—afraid to show yourself."

"Not afraid," a vaguely familiar voice replied.

"Then show yourself. Want to get this over with. My gun's holstered—we'll start even."

He was taking a long chance, Shawn knew. The killer could choose to remain hidden behind the shed and fire his weapon without exposing himself—and at such close range he could hardly miss. But Starbuck, the remembrance of Joe Fargo dying in his arms foremost in his mind, along with the recollection of the bushwhacker's earlier attempts to kill him from ambush, would have it no other way.

He had at last caught up with the man. There would be

no more looking over his shoulder, and the cause, whatever its source, would be settled here and now on one of Dodge City's back streets, along with payment exacted for the murder, intentional or not, of his friend.

"I'm through talking—step out or I'm coming in after you."

Starbuck's shoulders hunched. There was movement again. A shadowy figure eased into the light. Surprise rocked him. It was Hubbard's friend—Kent.

"You!" The words exploded from his lips. "Why the hell—"

Kent, arms hanging loosely at his sides, fingers spread wide, looked pale and strained in the lamp's glow.

"Name's Ivory—Kent Ivory. That mean anything to you?"

Ivory . . . Jim Ivory—a man he'd met and fought and killed in Arizona a time ago. Understanding came.

"It does. He was an outlaw. You're his brother, I take it."

"Right. Was living in Chicago when I got word he'd been murdered."

"Not murder. It was a fair fight."

"Murdered," Kent Ivory repeated dully. "Jim was the only relation I had, and I owe him plenty. Paid for my schooling, saw that I had money to live on while I learned a trade—and then you ended it all by—"

"Not my choice," Starbuck said quietly. "If you went to Lynchburg they told you that."

"Was there all right. Hung around several months hoping you'd come. You did—and a man in a restaurant pointed you out."

"He tell you about your brother, too? What he was mixed up in?"

"That doesn't matter. You killed him."

"After that you followed me, waiting to get your chance. Where does Hubbard come in?"

"Ran into him after I missed you the first time. Said there was a town on a ways that he was headed for. I guessed you were going to the same place, so I threw in with him. . . . That was Joe Fargo with you. Did I—I—"

"He's dead."

"It was an accident. Had nothing against him. My quarrel's with you."

"No quarrel far as I can see. All in the way you're thinking. I'm willing to ride back to Lynchburg and prove it to you."

"Wouldn't bring back Jim."

"Nothing will," Starbuck said.

He could see now how it could easily have been Kent and wondered why he hadn't realized it earlier. The poor handling of a gun, which would indicate a greenhorn; the times on the drive when Kent could have slipped off unnoticed by the other drovers and made his try. And that day before, during the confusion when the raiders struck, he had simply taken advantage of the dust, of all the shooting—and had come near to success.

But he knew now—and talking was getting him nowhere. There was no reasoning with the man.

"What's it to be?"

"I'm going to kill you—same as you did Jim."

"You'll never make it. You don't know how to use that gun you're wearing. Proved that several times."

"I can shoot. Maybe not so good at a distance, but close like this, I won't miss. Maybe you'll get me, but I'll get you, too."

Shawn considered Kent quietly. He was determined to go through with a shoot out and there was no dissuading him. But he was inexperienced and unskilled; he would have no chance. In defending himself, Shawn knew he would be committing murder—and he wanted none of that to haunt him for the rest of his life.

He was being given no choice, however. When Kent went for his pistol he could do nothing but draw and fire to protect himself. Starbuck's eyes narrowed. Perhaps there was an answer—not permit Kent Ivory to even go for his weapon. A man drawing fast to avoid death must trigger at the largest part of his target, not take time to aim in the hope of only wounding.

He didn't like the thought; it boiled down to taking advantage of an opponent, giving him no opportunity, sneaking in the first shot—but by degrading himself in that manner, Kent Ivory would not die.

Coming to his decision, Starbuck twisted slightly, turning his left side away from the man so that movement of his hand as it brought up his pistol would go unseen.

"Still think you're a fool," he said, and leveled the forty-five.

"You've got to pay for killing Jim—"

Ivory's words broke as he saw Starbuck take deliberate aim. He made a grab for the weapon on his hip. The night rocked once more with the blast of gunshot. Kent staggered, forgetting his gun, clawing at his shoulder.

"You—you never gave me a chance!" he screamed.

"You're a killer—a murderer, just like I said!"

Starbuck, holstering his weapon, stepped up to Ivory, and taking the man's pistol, tossed it aside.

"Maybe so," he said, "but you're still alive."

24

Boot heels were pounding along the street. Voices were shouting back and forth and the audience at the edge of the walk had increased. Shawn turned his attention to the group.

"There a doctor around close?"

"Never mind that," the first of two men wearing deputy marshal stars said, pushing through the crowd. "We'll tend to it."

They halted before Starbuck and Kent. The taller of the pair, a double-barreled shotgun leveled in his hands, glanced from one to the other and waited while his companion pulled Shawn's weapon from its holster and retrieved Ivory's from where it lay. Then, "What the hell's going on here?"

"The big one there," a voice volunteered from the crowd, "he just up and shot the other'n. They was talking, sort of arguing, when all of a sudden he comes up with his gun and shoots. Didn't give the little fellow a chance."

The deputy was staring coldly at Starbuck. "You know the law here in Dodge about wearing a gun—"

Shawn nodded. More people were gathering. A woman near the front said, "You hadn't ought to leave that boy standing there bleeding—"

"He'll live," the lawman cut in drily, and half turned as a man elbowed a path through the tight circle of onlookers and came forward. It was Fargo's friend, Glover. He squinted at Kent and then at Shawn.

"Got him, I see. Good!"

The deputy frowned. "What d'you know about this, Abe?"

"He killed Joe Fargo," the rooming-house owner said, pointing at Kent. "Then this other—"

The lawman swung to Kent. "That right?"

"Was an accident—"

The deputy came back to Glover. "You damn sure this Fargo's dead?"

"Course I am, Tuck! He's back there on my porch if you want to see for yourself. Died while Starbuck there was holding him."

Tuck lowered his weapon, fixing his eyes on Shawn. "That what caused the shooting? He gunned your friend and you went after him?"

"About it. Bullet was meant for me. Missed and hit Fargo."

"He wasn't packing no iron when it happened," Glover said. "Seen him get it out of his saddlebags after Joe was killed."

The tall deputy glanced at his fellow officer and shook his head. "Hell, let's take them both to the cooler and leave it up to Wyatt to sort it out. Give me their guns, then you best go after Doc Miller, have him meet us there."

The younger lawman handed over the two weapons and moved off into the night. Abe reached out, catching Tuck by the arm.

"Mind you, tell Earp what I said about Starbuck not carrying a gun. Went and got it only when he had to."

"All right, Abe, all right," Tuck said, motioning to Shawn and Kent to step out in front of him. "I hear. If Wyatt's needing help, he'll send for you."

They reached the jail and turned into it. Shawn nodded to the dark-faced lawman with flowing black mustache sitting behind the desk as they entered. Earp gave no sign of recognition, but only stared back, his eyes a cold, ice blue.

"These the ones doing the shooting?"

Tuck nodded and laid the two pistols on the desk. "Kind of a mixed-up thing. There's a jasper laying on Abe Glover's porch dead. Was him," the deputy jerked a thumb at Kent, "that done it, but he was shooting at this other fellow. Then that'n gets his gun out of his saddlebag, goes after this'n, wings him. . . . Mort's gone after the doc."

Earp was studying Shawn intently. "I know you?"

"Met a few months ago . . . name's Starbuck."

The lawman settled back. "Sure, you're the one that came here looking for somebody—your brother, I recollect it was. Then you went over and took the marshal job at Babylon."

"You've got a good memory."

"Pays to sometimes," Earp said laconically. "What's this all about?"

"Was the way the deputy told it."

"It's not the truth of it!" Ivory broke in bitterly. "He's a killer—murdered my brother!"

Earp folded his hands and considered Kent thoughtfully. "And you were out to get him for it. Took a shot at him in the dark and hit this—"

"Name was Joe Fargo," Tuck supplied.

Earp shifted his flat gaze to Shawn. "You kill his brother?"

"I did. Down in Arizona. He was an outlaw, and we had it out. You can get the story from the marshal, town called Lynchburg. His name's Huckaby."

Earp made no comment. Kent, hand still gripping his shoulder, face taut with pain, shook his head angrily.

"He's lying! My brother wasn't an outlaw—and even if he was, his killing was a murder. Like as not Starbuck didn't give him a chance, either."

The lawman frowned. "Either?"

"Didn't me. Kept me talking, and when I wasn't noticing, he drew his pistol and shot me."

Wyatt Earp's eyes narrowed in understanding. A wry smile pulled at his lips. "Friend, you got plenty to learn. I know this fellow, heard plenty about him when he was wearing a badge. He could have emptied his gun into you before you got through blinking if he'd wanted to. What he was doing was busting you up a little so's you couldn't force him to kill you. . . . That it, Starbuck?"

"Only way out," Shawn admitted.

"What you ought to be doing is thanking him for letting you live," the lawman continued. "There's a plenty of men, most I expect, who wouldn't have gone to all that trouble."

Kent Ivory was staring at Starbuck. "I won't believe that—"

"You're still alive," Earp said. "You can believe that,

can't you? That's all the proof you need. And far as your brother's concerned, I'll take Starbuck's word on that too, but if you figure that ain't enough, I can get off word to that marshal in Arizona and see what he has to say about it."

Kent looked down. "Already talked to him myself."

"Told you the same thing Starbuck did, that it?"

"He did—"

"But you wanted to put a bullet in Starbuck anyway, that it?"

"He was my brother—he was murdered—"

"Not exactly; and if Starbuck hadn't got him, somebody else would've. But you forget about him. You've got trouble of your own—charge of murder."

"That was an accident, Marshal," Shawn said hurriedly. "Fargo was a friend of his, too. Just happened to get in the way of a bullet aimed at me."

"Still, a man is dead—killed."

"I realize that, but seeing that Ivory's a stranger in this part of the country and was sort of off on the wrong track, I thought maybe you could let it pass as an accident if he'd give his word he'd go back where he belongs— Chicago. I think if Joe Fargo was around and had any say in it, he'd be for that."

Earp toyed with a tip of his mustache, eyes almost closed in thought. Abruptly he glanced up at Kent. "You agree to that?"

Ivory, staring at Starbuck, a puzzled look on his face, nodded slowly. "Yes, sir—"

"All right then," the lawman snapped. "I'm putting it down as an accident—and I'll be expecting you to catch the first train out of town soon as the doc fixes you up. Understand?"

"I'll be on it," Kent said, still facing Shawn. "I want to thank you—thank both of you. Guess I let things get out of hand, just thinking too hard about them. I'm sorry about it if I—"

"Forget it," Starbuck said, and turning to Earp, pointed at his pistol. "Be all right if I take my gun and move on?"

The lawman picked up the weapon by the barrel and passed it over, butt forward. "You know the law—don't wear it around here."

Shawn nodded. Then, "You got a man locked up by the name of Vance?"

"Reckon I have," Earp replied, and frowned. "You ain't the one he was trying to draw on are you?"

"I am. He was some liquored up."

"Some! I'd say it was more than a plenty. Grabbed a gun when the deputy brought him in here and tried to shoot me. Had to buffalo him. He's laying back there in a cell, out cold yet, I expect—and he's going to stay there for thirty more days. . . . How many jaspers you got gunning for you, anyway?"

"No more, far as I know. Vance'll be all right once he sobers up. Any chance you turning him loose on my say-so?"

Earp wagged his head. "Now, that's one thing I can't do, not after what he done." The lawman's cold eyes narrowed. "There some special reason why you want him out?"

"Not for a fight, if that's what you're thinking. He was with me on a drive, coming up from Texas. Just don't like to leave him here in trouble."

"He'll be all right, and I reckon he's old enough to find his way back home. When are you leaving town?"

"Got a little personal business to take care of with Abe Glover first, and I want to see to the burying of Joe Fargo. Then I'll be moving on."

"Still hunting that brother of yours, that it?"

"Still hunting," Starbuck said, and turned to the door.

Center Point Publishing
600 Brooks Road • PO Box 1
Thorndike ME 04986-0001 USA

(207) 568-3717

US & Canada:
1 800 929-9108